"Tomorrow you'll be pushin' grass from the under side," I said . . .

They stared at me. They were trying to figure whether I was all talk or whether I was tough. Me, I'm not backward about giving a man a chance. Many a time a man with whiskey in him is apt to talk too much, and suddenly realize he wished he was somewhere else. I was giving them this chance.

They didn't take it.

The long-geared man with the handlebar mustache looked at me and said, "I'm Arch Hadden," like he expected me to show scare at the name.

"Glad to meet you, Mr. Hadden," I said gently. "I'll carve the slab myself."

THE LONELY MEN

LOUIS L'AMOUR

BENDIGO SHAFTER
BORDEN CHANTRY
BOWDRIE
BOWDRIE'S LAW
BRIONNE
THE BROKEN GUN
BUCKSKIN RUN
THE BURNING HILLS
THE CALIFORNIOS
CALLAGHEN
CATLOW
CHANCY
THE CHEROKEE TRAIL
COMSTOCK LODE
CONAGHER
CROSSFIRE TRAIL
DARK CANYON
DOWN THE LONG HILLS
THE EMPTY LAND
FAIR BLOWS THE WIND
FALLON
THE FERGUSON RIFLE
THE FIRST FAST DRAW
FLINT
FRONTIER
GUNS OF THE TIMBERLANDS
HANGING WOMAN CREEK
HELLER WITH A GUN
THE HIGH GRADERS
HIGH LONESOME
THE HILLS OF HOMICIDE
HONDO
HOW THE WEST WAS WON
THE IRON MARSHAL
THE KEY-LOCK MAN
KID RODELO
KILKENNY
KILLOE
KILRONE
KIOWA TRAIL
LAW OF THE DESERT BORN
THE LONESOME GODS
THE MAN CALLED NOON
THE MAN FROM SKIBBEREEN
MATAGORDA
MILO TALON
THE MOUNTAIN VALLEY WAR
NORTH TO THE RAILS
OVER ON THE DRY SIDE
PASSIN' THROUGH
THE PROVING TRAIL

THE QUICK AND THE DEAD
RADIGAN
REILLY'S LUCK
THE RIDER OF LOST CREEK
RIVERS WEST
THE SHADOW RIDERS
SHALAKO
SHOWDOWN AT YELLOW
  BUTTE
SILVER CANYON
SITKA
SON OF A WANTED MAN
THE STRONG SHALL LIVE
TAGGART
TO TAME A LAND
TUCKER
UNDER THE SWEET-
  WATER RIM
UTAH BLAINE
THE WALKING DRUM
WAR PARTY
WESTWARD THE TIDE
WHERE THE LONG GRASS
  BLOWS
YONDERING

Sackett Titles by
Louis L'Amour

---

1. SACKETT'S LAND
2. TO THE FAR BLUE
   MOUNTAINS
3. THE DAYBREAKERS
4. SACKETT
5. LANDO
6. MOJAVE CROSSING
7. THE SACKETT BRAND
8. THE LONELY MEN
9. TREASURE MOUNTAIN
10. MUSTANG MAN
11. GALLOWAY
12. THE SKY-LINERS
13. THE MAN FROM THE
    BROKEN HILLS
14. RIDE THE DARK TRAIL
15. THE WARRIOR'S PATH
16. LONELY ON THE
    MOUNTAIN
17. RIDE THE RIVER
18. JUBAL SACKETT

LOUIS L'AMOUR
THE LONELY MEN

BANTAM BOOKS
TORONTO • NEW YORK • LONDON • SYDNEY • AUCKLAND

To the people of Schimmert,
in the province of Limburg,
The Netherlands,
who took into their homes
a company of American soldiers,
February 1945.

THE LONELY MEN

A Bantam Book / May 1969
2nd printing ..... May 1969   3rd printing ... October 1969
4th printing .... March 1970
New Bantam edition / April 1971

2nd printing ... August 1971	14th printing ..... June 1978
3rd printing . December 1971	15th printing ... January 1979
4th printing ..... April 1972	16th printing ... January 1979
5th printing ... October 1972	17th printing ..... May 1979
6th printing ... August 1973	18th printing ... March 1980
7th printing ... August 1974	19th printing ..... June 1980
8th printing ... October 1974	20th printing .. February 1981
9th printing . December 1975	21st printing ... August 1981
10th printing ..... May 1976	22nd printing ..... June 1982
11th printing . September 1976	23rd printing ..... April 1983
12th printing ..... April 1977	24th printing . November 1983
13th printing . September 1977	25th printing . September 1983

ISBN 0-553-25507-X

Published simultaneously in the United States and Canada

Bantam Books are published by Bantam Books, Inc. Its trademark, consisting of the words "Bantam Books" and the por-
trayal of a rooster, is Registered in U.S. Patent and Trademark
Office and in other countries. Marca Registrada. Bantam
Books, Inc., 666 Fifth Avenue, New York, New York 10103.

PRINTED IN THE UNITED STATES OF AMERICA

H   34 33 32 31 30 29 28

Chapter 1

IT WAS HOT. The shallow place where I lay atop the desert ridge was like an oven, the rocks like burning coals. Out on the flat below, where the Apaches waited, the heat waves shimmered and danced. Only the far-off mountains looked cool.

When I tried to push out my tongue to touch my cracked lips it was like a dry stick in my mouth, and the dark splashes on the rock were blood . . . my blood.

The round thing lying yonder with a bullet hole in it was my canteen, but there might be a smidgen of water left in the bottom—enough to keep me alive if I could get to it.

Down on the flat lay my sorrel horse, who had run himself to death trying to save my hide, and him with a bullet hole in his belly. In the saddlebags were the few odds and ends that were likely to be as much as I'd ever have of possessions in this life, for I didn't seem to be a fortunate man when it came to getting the riches of the world.

Back in the high-up Tennessee hills they used to tell it that when fighting time came around a body should stand clear of us Sacketts, but those Apaches down yonder had never heard the stories, and wouldn't have paid them no mind if they had.

If you saw an Apache on a parade ground he might not stack up too much, but out in the brush and rocks of his native country, he was a first-class fighting man, and maybe the greatest guerilla fighter the world ever saw.

Squinting my eyes against the glare and the thin trickle of salty sweat in my eyes, I clutched the stock of my rifle right back of the action and searched the terrain for something at which to shoot. My mouth was dry, my fingers stiff, and my rifle action so hot I daren't touch it unless to shoot, and quick.

Down there on the trail Billy Higgins lay gut-shot and dead, killed at the last by my own bullet to save him from torture.

We'd been riding east in the cool of the morning when those Apaches hit us from out of nowhere. Rightly, this wasn't even Apache country. This was Pima or Papago country, and they were Indians who were friendly to us, and who fought the Apaches on every occasion.

When those 'Paches hit us it was every man for himself, and Billy Higgins and me, we taken out a-running, heading for the rocks where we could make a fight of it.

An Apache with a .56 Spencer r'ared up from behind a greasewood and shot Billy right through the belly, opening him up as if it had been done with a saber. It meant he was dying, and he knew it.

Swinging my horse, I came back to him where he had fallen, but he looked up cool as could be and said, "You light out, Tell. I've seen some gut-shot folks in my time, but nobody had it worse than me."

The shock of the bullet was still on him, but in a minute or two he would begin to suffer.

When I got down to lift him up he stopped me. "Before God, Tell, if you try to pick me up everything I've got in me will spill out. You hit the trail, but try to get another one for me, will you? You can he'p more up in the rocks, keepin' them off me."

What he said was gospel true and we both knew it, so I swung my horse and lit a shuck for those rocks as if my sorrel's tail was afire. Only we didn't get far. I heard the shots and felt the sorrel's hoofs break rhythm, and then he started to cave under me, but somehow he fought himself up and kept on for fifty yards more. Then he started to go and I hit the ground running before he was down, with bullets kicking gravel ahead of and around me.

Almost at the top of the ridge a bullet caught me, and it saved my life.

It spun me, knocked me rolling butt over teakettle into the rocks, with two more bullets hitting right where I'd been. Scrambling up, I dove over into that shallow place and lay there, rifle in hand, hugging the ground. When the first Apache showed, I nailed him right between the eyes.

After that things quieted down, but there was no way to get clear. The ground around me hadn't anything in the way of cover, so I had to stay where I was . . . with the morning ebbing away into noontime.

I'd no idea how many Apaches were out there. As they lived off the desert they never traveled in big bunches; there were rarely as many as thirty, more often twelve to eighteen, so far as I'd seen or heard.

Off to the northwest I could hear shooting, time to time, so some of the others must be alive, after all. There'd been five of us, to start, and all strangers who met in Yuma. That was the way it was in those days. More often than not a man might find himself traveling with folks he'd never seen before. None of the five of us had any knowledge of the others before we hit the trail. Traveling alone was a mighty chancy thing in Indian country, so it was lucky that we all shaped up to go east at the same time.

Now Billy was down, but I'd nailed an Apache. Right at the moment my chances didn't look good. If they were settin' a place for me in Tucson they'd best wait, for it began to look like there'd be an empty spot at the table.

I hunkered down a mite and piled a few rocks on the edge of the hollow to give me some more protection, leaving a place here and there to look through or fire through. I took time to replace the shells I'd fired . . . no idea when the chance would come again.

Apaches are great waiters. They could set for hours on end, just waiting a wrong move. A white man, he gets restless, wants to move, and the first thing you know he does, and he dies.

Not me. I grew up in Cherokee country in Tennessee, and my pa had been a mountain man who'd fought Indians from boyhood . . . he'd taught us when he was home, taught us all he could, and I learned from the Indians, too.

This shallow place in which I lay was scarcely three feet deep. It was maybe eight feet each way, and the lowest part was where the run-off water had started a trench that emptied into a draw in back of me.

The sky was a hot yellow, the land pinkish, with outcroppings of dull red or black. There was mighty little growth—just scraggly desert shrubs and prickly pear, and mighty little of that.

The time inched by, with no change in the heat, no change in the sun, no change in the country around. Unless I lifted my head, nothing could be seen and I must trust to my hearing.

On the slope, there was nothing. My horse lay down there, and the body of Billy Higgins.

I hadn't been there long when I heard Billy scream. Taking a chance, I peeked out.

The Apaches were shooting flaming slivers of pitch pine into him with their bows. They were hidden down close to him, and there was no way I could get at them, nor them at me. They were shooting into Billy to torture him, which amused them, but also they were doing it to draw me out.

Three fires were smoldering in him before he screamed. And then he yelled to me: "Tell! For God's sake, Tell! Shoot me!"

He lay out on the white sand in the glare of the awful sun, ripped open by a bullet, and the Apaches kept shooting those little arrows of flaming pitch pine into him.

"Tell!"

There was terrible agony in his voice, and a pleading, too.

All of a sudden, he forced himsef up and he put a finger against his skull. "Tell! Right there! For God's sake, Tell!"

So I shot him. He would have done it for me.

You should have heard those Apaches yell. I'd spoiled their fun, and they were mad, real mad.

One of them jumped up, running at me, but just as I was about to shoot he dropped from sight; then another started and another, both disappearing before I could bring my rifle to bear, but each one a few yards closer.

Times like that, a body does some thinking, and right then I was a-wishing I was somewhere else, a-wishing I'd never come to Arizona a-tall, although until then I'd been mighty proud of the Territory, and even though hard times had come upon me I liked the country. Right now all I wanted was a way out . . . any way out. But those Apaches had a mind to keep me there.

All of a sudden one of them came up out of the sand and started for me, but when I swung my gun, another started up.

Now, even a fool boy from the hills is going to learn after a while, and so the next time one started up I didn't swing my gun and try to nail him, I just waited with my eyes on the place where the first one dropped. Not exactly on the place, for no Apache will ever get up from where he drops; he rolls over a few feet to right or left, sometimes quite a few feet.

Another of them started up, but I let him come until he dropped. and I waited for the first one. Sure enough, up he bobbed and I had to move the rifle muzzle only inches, and I nailed him right in the brisket, dusting him on both sides. Before he could fall I worked the lever on my Winchester and got him again.

Then the others were coming and, swinging the gun, I caught another one . . . too low down. He hit the ground in the open and the third one also dropped, not more than twenty feet now from the rim of my hollow.

One lay out there with what looked like a busted leg,

and I let him lay until he tried to bring his rifle to bear, and then I eased around for a shot at him. The muzzle of my rifle must have showed a mite beyond the rocks at the edge of my hole, because the third one fired, hitting the rocks and spattering me with stinging rock fragments, one of which took me right in the eye.

Then they came, the two of them. The one with the bloody but unbroken leg, and the third one shooting as he came. I dropped my rifle and, with my eyes full of water from the smart of rock fragments, grabbed my bowie knife.

Now, I'm a pretty big man, standing six foot three in my socks, and although on the lean side what beef I had was packed into my arms and shoulders. That bowie knife was a heavy blade, razor-sharp, and when those two 'Paches jumped into the hollow with me I took a wicked swipe at where they figured to be. Somebody screamed, and I felt a body smash against me. Upping my knee. I threw him off and fell back, just missing a slashing blow that would have taken my head off.

One Apache was down but not out. I could see a little now, and when I started to come up he grabbed at my rifle which was lying there and I threw myself at him, knocking the barrel aside with one hand and ripping up with that blade with the other.

He threw me off and I fell, all sprawled out, and they both came up and at me. One had a wounded leg, one had a slash across the chest and biceps, but they were tigers, believe me. It was like being in a mess of wildcats, and for the next thirty or forty seconds I never knew which end was up, until of a sudden the fight was over and I was lying there on the ground, gasping for breath, with tearing gasps.

Finally I pushed myself up from the sand and turned over into a sitting position.

One Apache was dead, my bowie knife still in his chest. I reached over and pulled it loose, watching the other one. He was lying there on his back and he had a bullet hole in his thigh that was oozing blood and he had at least three knife cuts, one of them low down on his right side that looked mean.

Reaching over, I taken up my rifle and jacked a shell into the chamber.

That 'Pache just kept a-staring at me; he seemed to be paralyzed, almost, for he made no move. The other two were dead.

Jerking a cartridge belt from one of the dead ones I looped it around my middle, still keeping an eye on the living one. Then I picked up my bowie knife from the ground and, leaning over to the living one I wiped off the blood on him, then stuck the knife into the scabbard.

One by one I collected their rifles and emptied the shells, then threw them wide.

"You're too good a fightin' man to kill," I told him. "You're on your own."

I walked down to where my canteen lay and picked it up. Sure enough, there was maybe a cup of water that had not drained out, and I drank it, watching the rim of the hollow all the while.

By now it was coming on to sundown and there were other Indians about. I took one more look into the hollow and that one was still lying there, although he'd tried to move. I could see a big rock back of his neck that maybe he'd hit across when he fell.

Taking a careful look around, I went down into the shallow gully left by the run-off water and started away.

About that time I found myself going lame. My hip and leg were mighty sore, and when I looked down to size the situation up I saw that a bullet had hit my cartridge belt, fusing two of my .44's together, and a fragment had gone up and hit my side, just a scratch, but it was bloody. That bullet that hit my belt where it crossed the hip had bruised me mighty bad, by the feel of it.

Shadows were creeping out from the rocks, and of a sudden it was cool and dark.

A voice spoke out. "You want to live long in this country you better get shut of them spurs."

It was Spanish Murphy. He came up from behind

some brush with Rocca and John J. Battles. Taylor was dead.

Murphy had lost the lobe of his left ear, and Rocca had been burned a couple of times, but no more.

"You get any?" Battles asked.

"Four," I said, knowing that was more Apaches than many an Indian fighter got in a lifetime. "Three, and a possible," I corrected. And then I added, "They got Billy."

"We'd best light out," Spanish suggested, and we walked single file to where their horses were. They had two horses, so we figured to switch off and on.

Spanish was tall as me, but twenty pounds lighter than my one-ninety. He was a reading man, always a-reading. Books, newspapers, even the labels on tin cans . . . anything and everything.

We set out then. After a while I rode Tampico Rocca's horse and he walked. By daybreak both horses were tired out and so were we, but we had sixteen miles behind us and a stage station down on the flat before us.

We were still several hundred yards off when a man walked from the door with a rifle in his hands, and we were almighty sure there was another one behind a window from the way he kept out of line with it.

When we came up to the yard he looked at Murphy, then at the rest of us, and back at Murphy. "Hello, Spanish. What was it? Apaches?"

"Have you got a couple of horses?" I asked him. "I'll buy or borrow."

"Come on inside."

It was cool and still. Me, I dropped into the first chair I saw and put my Winchester on the table.

A second man left the window where he had been keeping watch and, carrying his rifle, he went back toward the kitchen, where he began rattling pots and pans. The first man went over to a table and carried the wooden bucket and the gourd dipper to us. "I'd go easy, there at first," he suggested. And that we did.

The station tender leaned on the bar. "Haven't seen

you in years, Spanish. Figured they'd have stretched
your neck before now."

"Give 'em time," John J. Battles said.

Setting there in the chair, taking occasional swallows
of cool water from the bucket, I began to feel myself
getting back to normal.

Spanish, he leaned back in his chair and looked over
his cup at the station tender. "Case, how long you been
with the Comp'ny?"

"Two . . . maybe two and a half years. My wife lef'
me. Said this western country was no place for a woman. She went back to her folks in Boston. I sent her
money, time to time. Afraid if I don't she'll come back
on me."

"Ain't never married, myself," Spanish said. He
looked over at me. "How about you, Tell?"

For a moment there I hadn't anything to say. I kept
thinking of Ange, the last times I saw her, and of the
first times, high in those Colorado mountains.

"My wife is dead," I told him. "She was a rarely fine
girl . . . rarely fine."

"Tough," Spanish said. "You, Rocca?"

"No, señor. I am not a married man. There was a
girl . . . but that is far away and long ago, *amigos*. Her
father had many cows, many horses . . . me, I had
nothing. And I was an Indio . . . my mother was an
Apache," he added.

My eyes were on the floor, tracing the cracks in the
rough boards, often scrubbed. My hungry flesh was
soaking up the lost moisture and I felt sleepy and quiet,
liking the square of sunlight that lay inside the door,
even the drone of the flies . . . I was alive.

The blood of Apaches was still on my hands. There
had been no water in which to wash until now, but soon
I would . . . soon.

The room was like many of its kind, differing only in
the plank floor. Most floors were of stamped earth.
There were several rough board tables, some chairs and
benches. The room was low-raftered, the walls were of

adobe, the roof of poles and earth. I could smell bacon frying in the kitchen, and coffee.

Spanish Murphy hitched around in his chair. "Tell, we make a team, the four of us, why don't we stick together?"

The man came in from the kitchen with tin plates and a frying pan filled with bacon. He dumped the plates on the table, then forked bacon onto them. He went out and returned with the coffeepot and a plate of *tortillas*. Still another trip and he brought a big bowl of *frijoles*—those big Mexican brown beans—and a dried-apple pie cut into four pieces.

"We'll need a couple of horses," I said, looking around at Case.

"You'll get 'em," Case replied. "I think the Comp'ny would like to get them to a safer place. We've been expectin' an attack almost any time."

He gestured toward the bacon. "You got to thank Pete Kitchen for the bacon. He raises hogs down to his place, calls 'em his 'Pache pincushions, they're so shot full of arrows."

John J. Battles, a solid chunk of a man, glanced across the table at me. "Sackett . . . that's a familiar name."

"I'm familiar," I agreed, "once you know me." It wasn't in me to get him comparing notes, figuring out who I was. Once he did, he'd bring up the fight in the Mogollon country, and how Ange was murdered. It was something I was wishful of forgetting.

"I still figure," Spanish said, "that we'd make a team."

"If you want to risk hanging." John J. Battles grinned at us. "You all heard what Case said."

"Me," Rocca said, "I wasn't going nowhere, anyhow."

"Later," I said, "it will have to be later. I've got a trip to take."

They looked at me, all of them. "My brother's kid. I hear tell he's been taken by the Apaches. I've got to go into the Sierra Madres after him."

They thought I was crazy, and I was thinking so my-self. Rocca was the first one to speak. "Alone? Señor, an army could not do it. That is the Apache hide-out where no white man goes."

"It's got to be done," I said.

Case, he just looked at me. "You're crazy. You're scrambled in the head."

"He's just a little boy," I said, "and he's alone down yonder. I think he will be expectin' somebody to come for him."

Chapter 2

LAURA SACKETT was a strikingly pretty young woman, blonde and fragile. Among the dark, sultry beauties of Spanish descent she seemed a pale, delicate flower, aloof, serene, untouchable.

To the young Army officers in the Tucson vicinity, Laura Sackett was utterly fascinating, and this feeling was not dulled by the knowledge that she was a married woman. Her husband, it was known, was Congressman Orrin Sackett, who was in Washington, D.C. Apparently they had separated.

But nobody seemed to know just what the status of the marriage was, and Laura offered no comment, nor did she respond to hints.

Her conduct was irreproachable, her manner lady-like; her voice was soft and pleasant. The more discerning did notice that her mouth was a little too tight, her eyes shadowed with hardness, but these characteristics were usually lost in the quiet smiles that hovered about her lips.

Nobody in Tucson had ever known Jonathan Pritts, Laura's father, and none of them had been present in the vicinity of Mora during the land-grant fighting.

Jonathan Pritts was now dead. A narrow, bigoted man, tight-fisted and arrogant, he had been idolized by his daughter and only child, and with his death her hatred for the Sacketts had become a fierce, burning urge to destroy.

She had seen her father driven from Mora, his dream

12

of empire shattered, his hired gunmen killed or imprisoned. A vain, petty, and self-important man, he had impressed upon his daughter that he was all the things he assumed he was, and to her all other men were but shadows before the reality of her father.

Until he had come west, they had lived together in genteel poverty. His schemes for riches had failed one by one, and with each failure his rancor and bitterness grew. Each failure, he was positive, had come not from any mistake on his part, but always from the envy or hatred of others.

Laura Pritts had married Orrin Sackett with one thought in mind—to further her father's schemes. Orrin, big, handsome, and genial, and fresh from the Tennessee hills, had never seen a girl like Laura. She seemed everything he had ever dreamed of. Tyrel had seen through her at once, and through her father as well, but Orrin would not listen. He was seeing what he wished to see—a great lady, a princess almost—graceful, alluring, a girl of character and refinement. But in the end he saw her, and her father, for what they were, and he had left her. And now Laura Pritts Sackett was returning, without a plan, without anything but the desire to destroy those who had destroyed her father.

As if by magic, on the stage to Tucson, the pieces began to fall into place. At the first stage stop east of Yuma she overheard the driver talking to the station tender.

"Saw him in Yuma," the driver was saying. "I'd have known him anywhere. Those Sackett boys all look alike."

"Sackett? The gunfighter?"

"They're all good with their guns. This one is Tell Sackett. He's been out California way."

The idea came to her that night. She had been trying to think of some way to hurt the Sacketts, to get even with them. Now here was Tell Sackett, the older brother, the one she had never met. It was unlikely that he knew of her difficulties with Orrin. The Sacketts wrote few letters, and from what she remembered Orrin had not seen his brother in years. Of course, he might have seen him since she left; but there was a chance, and she resolved to take it.

The means was supplied to her also by way of a conversation overheard. She had heard many such conversations without thinking of how they might be used. The men were talking of the Apaches, of some children stolen by them, perhaps killed. "Two of them were Dan Creed's boys. I don't know who the other one was."

The young Army lieutenant on the stage had made tentative efforts at a conversation with Laura, all of which she had studiously avoided. At his next attempt she surprised him by turning with a faint, somewhat remote smile.

"Is it true, Lieutenant, that there are Apaches about? Tell me about them."

Lieutenant Jack Davis leaned forward eagerly. He was a very young man, and Laura Sackett was a beautiful young woman. It was true he had himself been on only two scouts into Apache country, but he had served with older, more experienced men who had talked freely, and he had listened well.

"Yes, there are Apaches," he said, "and it is true we might encounter them at any time, but the men on this coach are all armed, and are experienced fighting men. You will not need to worry."

"I was not worried about them, Lieutenant, merely curious. Is it true that when attacked they retreat into Mexico? Into the Sierra Madre?"

"Unfortunately, yes. And the Mexicans are not helpful. They refuse to allow any of our armed forces to cross the border in pursuit, although I believe there are some indications the two governments may work together against the Apaches."

"So it seems likely that if a prisoner were taken over the border into Mexico you would not have much chance of recovering him, would you?"

"Almost none. A few times exchanges have been arranged. In a few cases individuals have traded goods or horses for a prisoner; but if the Apaches are pursued, they usually kill their prisoners."

Laura Pritts Sackett was thoughtful, and at the next stage stop she wrote her note to William Tell Sackett. Unless she was completely mistaken, he would come to Tucson at once; and unless she was equally mistaken, he would start at once for the Sierra Madres. The rest would be up to the Apaches.

What the Apaches failed to do, if they failed, might be done by other means . . . for which the Apaches would receive due credit.

Skillfully, she drew out the young lieutenant, and his comments were added to from time to time by one or another of the coach passengers. By the time the stage arrived in Tucson, Laura was well posted on the activities of the Apaches in Arizona Territory, as well as on the many times they had killed or kidnaped children, from the Oatman Massacre to the moment of her stage trip.

"Supposing one man or several men—not soldiers—were to try to go into the Sierra Madres?" she asked Lieutenant Davis.

"They would never return alive." The lieutenant was positive. "They wouldn't have a chance."

One of the passengers, a bleak, hard-faced man in rough frontier garb, looked around at him briefly. "Depend on the man," he said after a moment, but if he was heard his comment was not acknowledged.

That night, seated before her mirror, Laura Sackett knew she had found what she wanted. To trap his beloved brother would be just as satisfying as to trap Orrin himself, or Tyrel, whom she blamed even more.

She wished only for one thing: to see their faces when they realized how their brother had been duped.

When that man at the stage station in Yuma told me there was a letter for me I thought he was surely mistaken. Why, I couldn't recall getting more than three or four letters in my whole life, and nobody knew I was in Yuma—nobody at all.

None of us folks had been much hand to write. Orrin and Tyrel had learned to write, but with me writing was an almighty slow affair, and not one to be undertaken lightly. And we were never much on just exchanging letters unless there was something all-fired important. But sure enough, this letter was for me, William Tell Sackett. It read:

> Dear Tell:
>   Our son, Orrin's and mine, has
> been taken by the Apaches. Orrin is in
> Washington, D.C. Tyrel is laid up.
>   Can you help me?
>   Laura Sackett

So old Orrin had him a boy! Now, nobody had seen fit to tell me, but drifting place to place the way I'd been, it was no wonder. And no need for me to know, when it came to that.

None of the family knew where I was, but that need cut no ice now. When I'd needed help the whole lot of them had come a-running, and if the Apaches had Orrin's boy I'd have to move fast before they killed him . . . if they hadn't already.

A body never knew what the Apaches would do. They might kill a child right off, or they might cotton to the youngster and raise him like one of their own sons, and with just as much affection and care. A lot depended on how old the boy was, on how he reacted, and on how fast the Apaches had to move.

The Apaches, I knew, had respect for the brave. They had no use for weakness or cowardice, and you'd get nothing but contempt by asking for mercy.

An Apache admired the virtues he himself needed in the life he led. Bravery, fortitude, endurance, and the skills of the hunter and the hunted—these were important to him, these he understood.

Tucson lay still under a hot noonday sun when we dusted our hocks down the main drag, eyes open for a saloon or an eating house where there'd be shade, something to wet our whistles, and the trail gossip we were eager to hear.

We rode into town with care, for we were all men with enemies. We rode with our guns loose in the holsters, ready to run or fight, as the case might be; but the street was empty, heavy with heat.

The temperature was over a hundred in the shade.

"All this town needs," John J. Battles said, "is more water and a better class of people."

"That's all hell needs," Spanish replied. "Let's get into the shade."

We were hard and lonely men who rode a hard and lonely way. We had known nothing of each other until this ride began in Yuma, and even now we knew scarcely more. But we had sweated and thirsted together, we had hungered and fought, and eaten trail dust together; so now we rode as brothers ride.

We were men with sorrows behind us, and battles too; men with regrets behind us of which we did not speak, nor too often think. With none to share our sorrows or regrets, we kept them to ourselves, and our faces were impassive. Men with no one to share their feelings learn to conceal those feelings. We often spoke lightly of things which we took very seriously indeed.

We were sentimental men, but that was our secret, for an enemy who knows your feelings is an enemy who has a hold on you. Not all poker is played over a card table.

Although we spoke so lightly of Tucson we all liked the town, and were glad to be there.

Me, I was nothing but a tall boy from the high-up Tennessee hills who tried to live the way he'd been taught. Ma hadn't much book learning, but she had straight-out ideas on what was fair and decent, and there was no nonsense about her and pa when it came to dealing with enemies, or those who were evil.

Pa stood by the same principles ma did, but pa taught us other things too: how to stand up for what he believed was right, and to back down for no man when it came to fighting time. He taught us how to fight, how to find our way through rough country, and how to handle cards better than most gamblers, although he didn't hold with gambling.

"If you go among the Philistines," he used to say, "it is better to go armed."

So he taught us how to recognize a bottom deal, and to read marked cards, and how the sharpers operated.

The four of us split up on the street in Tucson. Rocca had some friends in the Mexican town, and Spanish Murphy went with him. John J. Battles had plans of his own, and so had I.

With me there was no choice, and little time. I met an idea head-on, and this time I had to do whatever might be done for that boy of Orrin's. I'd get cleaned up, get a bite to eat, and then I'd find this Laura Sackett.

I'd never met Orrin's wife, but any woman Orrin would cotton to would be all right with me. I'd been away from the other boys and knew little of their affairs. Tyrel had married a girl of Spanish blood, and had done well. Orrin had run for office and been elected, and I did recall some talk of his marrying, but none of the details. Nor had I any idea why she was in Tucson, and him in Washington. Folks' affairs are their own business, and I never was one for asking questions. What folks wanted me to know they would tell me, and I had enough to keep me busy.

The Shoo-Fly Restaurant was a long, narrow room with a white muslin ceiling and a floor of rammed earth. There were a few windows, a dozen or so tables of pine boards, and some chairs and benches, none of which would set quite even on the floor, but the food was good, and it was a cool, quiet place after the desert.

When I ducked through the door and straightened up inside, it taken me a moment to get my eyes accustomed to the place.

Three Army officers sat at one table, two older men and their wives at another. John Titus and a man named Bashford, both important men in the community, sat nearby. At a table in the corner near the window sat a blonde young woman, pale and pretty, her parasol beside her. When I came in she looked at me quick and puzzled, then glanced away.

Seemed like I was the roughest-dressed man in the place, and the biggest. My boots were down at heel, and my big California-style spurs rattled when I walked. My jeans were 'most wore out, and they carried a blood stain. I'd shaved, all right, but my hair was long and shaggy, and of course I was packing a six-shooter as well as a bowie knife, and carrying a Winchester.

Mrs. Wallen, who ran the place, remembered me from a while back. "How do you do, Mr. Sackett," she said. "Did you just get in?"

"Four of us did," I said dryly. "Two of us didn't."

Titus looked around at me. "Apaches?"

"Uh-huh . . . I'd say about fifteen, twenty of them."

"Get any of them?"

"Some," I said, and took a seat at a table near the wall where I could see the door and could stand my rifle in a corner.

"If you got any," one of the Army officers said, "you were lucky."

"I was lucky," I said.

Mrs. Wallen, who knew hungry men, as any frontier woman would, was already at the table with a cup and a pot of coffee. Then she brought me a slab of beef and some chili and beans, regular fare for that country.

As I ate, my muscles relaxed. A man on the run or fighting can get himself all keyed up with muscle and nerve ready for trouble until he's tighter than a drumhead. This was a pleasant room, and while I was never much hand for mixing in society, I liked folks, and liked to be among them.

Orrin was the mixer of the family. He had him an easy way with folks, he liked to talk and to listen, and he played a guitar and sang like any good Welshman. Give him ten minutes in a room and he'd be friends with everybody there.

Me, I was quiet. I guess I'm friendly enough, but I was never much hand at getting acquainted with folks.

I figure I was shaped to be a wallflower, but I don't mind. I sort of like to set back and listen to folks, to drink coffee, and contemplate.

When trouble shaped up, Orrin would try to talk a man out of it, although he was a hand at any kind of fighting when they decided not to listen. Tyrel, he was the mean one. I mean he was a fine man, but you couldn't push him. He just hadn't any give in him at all. If you come to Tyrel a-hunting after trouble he had plenty to offer. Me, I wasn't much of a talker, and no kind of a trouble-hunter. Folks had to bring it to me hard, but when they did that I just naturally reacted.

I'd roped and hogtied many a wild longhorn out on the plains of Texas, and I'd busted some mustangs in my time, and quite a few hard-to-get-along-with men, too. When it came to shooting, well, me and Tyrel could never figure which was best. We had both been shooting since we were big enough to lift a cartridge.

Sitting there in that quiet room, my muscles resting easy and the warmth of food stealing through me, I listened to the talk around and wondered if ever I would have a home of my own. Seemed as if every chance left me with less than before.

My home was wherever I hung my hat, but these here were mostly settled folks out for a bite to eat on a Sunday, which this was. Back in the mountains, come Sunday we used to dress in our go-to-meetin' clothes and drive down to church.

It was a fine old get-together in those days. We'd listen to the preacher expounding of our sins, most of us kind of prideful we'd managed to sin so much, but ashamed before his tongue-lashing, and some were kind of amazed that they were so sinful after all. Seemed like with farming and cussing the mules, a body didn't rightly find much time for sinning.

We'd sing the hymns in fine, rolling, and sometimes out-of-tune voices, and after church we'd set out under the trees with our picnic lunches and some of the womenfolks would swap food back and forth. Emmy Tatum, she made the best watermelon pickles any place around, and old Jeannie Bland from up at the forks of the creek, she could make apple cider that would grow bark on a mushroom.

That was long ago and far away, but sometimes I could set back and close my eyes and still hear those folks a-singing "On Jordan's Stormy Banks" or "Rock of Ages," or maybe the one about the church in the wildwood. Everything was homemade, even the clothes we wore. Why, I'd been nigh to sixteen before I ever saw a pair of store-bought pants, or shoes we hadn't cobbled ourselves out of our own tanned leather.

One of the Army officers was standing beside my table. "Mind if I sit down, sir?" he said.

"Welcome," I said. "My name is Sackett, William Tell Sackett."

He extended his hand. "Captain Lewiston, sir. You mentioned a difficulty with the Apaches. Did you get a good look at any of them?"

"Well, they weren't reservation Indians, if that's what you mean."

"How do you know that?"

Me, I just looked at him. "By the smell of them. They'd come out of the desert after a long ride. The droppings of their horses showed fibers of desert plants they'd eat only if there was nothing else."

"Did you say you got some of them?"

"Three . . . and one I hurt but didn't kill."

He looked at me, and so I told him. "He was too good a fighting man to kill, Captain. I got two of them with my rifle, and then two jumped me in the hollow. One I killed, but the other was a tiger. He seemed to have been paralyzed so I let him lay."

"You weren't alone?"

"Three men along with me, but not right there. I think they might have killed some, too."

"You lost two men?"

"Taylor and Billy Higgins. I never knew Taylor's first name. We didn't get a chance to pick up their bodies. When we could pull out, we did."

"About the dead ones, now. Did one of them have a

scar on his cheekbone? That would be just too much to expect, I suppose."

"No . . . not the dead ones. I didn't notice any scars on the dead one. But that one I left alive, he had a scar on his cheekbone."

Chapter 3

CAPTAIN LEWISTON SIGHED. "You may wish you had killed him, Mr. Sackett. That was Kahtenny, one of the most dangerous and elusive Apaches of them all."

"He was in pretty bad shape, Captain, and I'm no man to kill a fighter like that when he's down and helpless."

Lewiston smiled. "I feel the same, but I am afraid there are some who do not. There are those who feel they all should be killed."

That there blonde girl across the room was sure enough listening, although she was making quite a show of doing nothing but sort of idling over her food.

"Captain, I fought those Indians because they attacked me. I don't blame them for that. The Apache has made fighting his way of living for as long as his oldest people can recall. Or as long as the oldest Pimas and Papagos recall.

"The way I figure it, they fight because it's their way, and we fight back because it's our way. Somebody wins, somebody loses. Nobody in this country, or anywhere that I know of, can live in peace unless he's got somebody somewhere, protecting him."

Mrs. Wallen brought the Captain some coffee, and we sat there a few minutes more, discussing the Apache and his ways.

"You've been a soldier, Mr. Sackett?"

"Yes, sir. I served four years during the War Between

the States. I was at Shiloh and the Wilderness . . . and a few other places."

"We could use you here. Ever thought of joining up again?"

"No. I did what I had to do when the time came to do it. Now I'll fight when somebody can't be persuaded to leave me alone. Seems to me I've done enough Indian fighting without joining up to hunt for it."

"Are you related to Congressman Sackett?"

"Brother. Fact is, I'm here to talk to his wife."

I glanced across the room at the blonde girl, who was now looking right at me. "I figure to get their son back from the Apaches."

"Their son?" Lewiston looked puzzled, but before he could say more, Laura Sackett interrupted.

"Tell? I am Laura Sackett. Will you join me?"

So I got up. "Excuse me, Captain," I said, and taking my coffee I walked over to her table.

"Howdy, ma'am. Seems strange, not knowing you, but when you and Orrin married I was clean across the country. Never heard much about it."

"Sit down, Tell. We must talk." She put her hand on mine and looked at me with those wide blue eyes. "Let's not talk about trouble now, Tell. I want to know about you. After all, we must get to know each other."

Now, there isn't much that's more likely to make a man talk than a pretty woman who is ready to listen, so I found myself a-talking to her, mostly about Ange and how I found her high up in those far Colorado mountains where nobody lived, and then how she was murdered and how I hunted down the killer and got myself in a tight spot.

She had a pretty smile, and she gave me a lot of it. There were a couple of things about her looks that I didn't really shape up to like, but nobody is perfect. She had a small mouth, and it was kind of tight and hard at times, but she was a pleasure to talk to, and I talked.

Finally, she said would I walk her home, and it came to me suddenly that we'd talked the afternoon away and those Army officers were gone. Once out of the restaurant, she told me about the boy Orry, as she called him.

"He was taken with the Creed boys," she explained, "and the Army can do nothing. I know if Orrin were here he would ride right down into Mexico and bring him back, but by the time Orrin could get here it might be too late. Then I heard you were in Yuma. You were my only chance."

"How old is the boy?"

"He's five . . . going on six." She paused. "I must warn you, Tell, whatever you decide to do, you must not mention it around here. The Army would not allow you to cross the border on any such mission. Right now they are trying to arrange a working agreement with the Mexicans to join forces in stamping out the Apaches. They want to attack them right in their stronghold in the Sierra Madre . . . and that's another reason we must hurry. I have heard that if the Apaches are attacked they will kill all their captives."

Shortening my pace, I walked beside her. There was small chance the boy was alive, but I could not tell her that. Not that I even gave thought to not going to hunt for him. We Sacketts stand by one another, come hell or high water. The boy was a Sackett, and he was my brother's son.

My mind went down that trail into Mexico, and I had a cold feeling along my spine. Every inch of that trail would be trouble, and not only from the Apaches. Water was scarce, and whilst the folks were friendly, the Rurales and the Army were not. They'd likely shoot a man out of hand.

Somewhere along the trail I'd heard about Dan Creed's two boys and another youngster being taken, but I hadn't any details, and they weren't important now.

A body would have to be almighty cautious. If the Army got wind of anyone going into Mexico with any such notion that would be the end of it. They'd surely stop him.

With negotiations going on between the two governments that would be all it would take to end them . . . they'd never believe he'd come into Mexico on his own.

My name being Sackett, and all, they might be suspicious. I mean the Army might.

And Laura made me uneasy. I'd no knowledge of womenfolks, and never had been able to talk to any but Ange. Other women left me tongue-tied and restless; and Laura, she was all white lace, blonde hair, and those dainty little lacy gloves with no fingers in them. And that parasol she carried . . . I was a raw country boy from the hills, not used to such fixings.

"You will try, then?" We had stopped at her door, and she rested her hand on my arm. "Tell, you're my only hope. There is no one else."

"I'll do what I can." Standing there on the step, with her a-looking at me from those big blue eyes, it made me wish I was three men, so as I could do more. "Don't you forget, ma'am, there's no accounting for Apaches. They're mighty notional when it comes to prisoners. You mustn't be hoping for much."

"He's such a little boy."

It came on me to wonder if she'd any notion what she was letting me in for, but I pushed the thought away. I had no call to be thinking of myself. How could she know what that trail into Sonora was like? A trail like a walk through hell, with ugly death waiting on every side, at every moment. You had to travel trails like that to know them. In my mind's eye I could see the faint thread of it winding across the hot desert under a brassy sky, with the sand underfoot and all kinds of cactus and thorny bush around, with rattlers and Gila monsters and all . . . to say nothing of outlaws and Indians.

A thought came to me suddenly. "I was wondering how Orrin ever let you get so far from him? You and the boy?"

She smiled quickly, sadly. "It was my father, Tell. He died in California and I had to go there for the funeral. There was no one else. When I found how dangerous it was, I left Orry here . . . I thought he'd be safe here."

That made sense, all right. Still, there was a lot that puzzled me, but a man could waste any amount of time quibbling and fussing over details, which was never my way. If anything was to be done it had to be done fast. With her description of the boy and his clothing, I decided I'd best get together an outfit and pull out.

She stood there, her white dress like a light against the adobe walls. I looked back once as I walked away, and she was still standing there, looking after me.

It worried me some because this whole thing had come on me so sudden that I'd no chance to sort of think things through. Out there on the trail with those Apaches around there'd been no time, and now it seemed there was no time either. Nevertheless, there was some thinking I had to do.

The worst of it was I was almighty short of money, and no matter what a man sets out to do, it seems it costs him something. This here was going to cost money as well as sweat, and maybe blood.

All I had to my name was about two hundred saved-up dollars, the most I'd had in months, and I'd lost my saddle back yonder, and needed a horse. We'd come into Tucson on horses just borrowed from the stage outfit, and they'd be going back soon.

So I needed a horse and an outfit, and a pack horse if I had enough to handle it.

What I wanted was a good used saddle, and there was a reason. I was of no mind to ride into Apache country with a squeaky new saddle. Now, any saddle will squeak a mite, and it's a comforting sort of sound, most times; but when there are Apaches around any sound more than your breathing is liable to get you killed.

I needed not only a saddle, but also, a pair of saddle-bags, a canteen, a poncho, a blanket, a spare cartridge belt and a small amount of grub. I'd have to live off the country, on food I could get without shooting. From the time I crossed the border I was going to have to move like a ghost.

Tampico Rocca was in the Quartz Rock Saloon when I came in, and I went to his table and sat down. He leaned across the table. "John J., he rides out tonight. There is trouble, I think."

"Trouble?"

"There was difficulty in Texas. Battles won out. Two of the dead man's brothers are in town, with some friends. Battles wants no more trouble."

"He's broke, isn't he?" Me, I dug down in my jeans. "I'm outfitting for Mexico, but I can let him have twenty dollars."

Rocca shook his head. "This is not what I mean, *amigo*. He will meet us outside of town. He wished me to tell you this so you would not think he rode off alone. We are coming with you, *señor*."

"Now, you see here. This is my affair, and you boys got no call to ride along. It's going to be rough."

Tampico chuckled. *"Amigo,* you talk to Rocca, not to some pilgrim. I am Rocca, who is half Apache and who has lived with them. I know where they go. I know how they live. You will need me, *amigo."*

Well, I just sat there, finding nothing to say. Words just don't come easy to me, and at such times I find myself coming up empty. So I just looked at him and he grinned and waved for another beer.

The place was filling up, and it was a tough place. Nobody ever said the Quartz Rock was gentle. Over at the Congress Hall Saloon you'd find the gentry. You'd find the solid men, the good men, and mixed with them some of the drifters, but the Quartz Rock was rough. At least when Foster ran it.

You drank their liquor and you took your chances at the games, and the men who hung out there were hard cases, men with the bark on, men who had been born with the bark on. There were men came into that place so rough they wore their clothes out from the inside first. When you saw a man walk into the Quartz Rock wearing a six-shooter or a bowie knife he wasn't wearing it for show.

We were finishing our second beer when four men came into the place.

Rocca sat up easily and moved on the chair to keep his gun hand free. This was beginning to shape up like grief of some kind, and I was in no mood for it.

They were four of a kind, raw and rugged, just in off the trail and they looked it. Like uncurried wolves they bellied up to the bar, and when they had had a drink, they looked around.

"It is those who seek for John J., *amigo*. I think they know I am his friend."

They crossed the room, the four of them, and every man-jack in the room could smell the trouble they brought with them.

They came to our table and ranged themselves in front of it. All of them were armed, and they wore guns as if they knew how to use them.

Me, I just sort of shifted one foot. The other foot was propped up on a chair's edge, resting easy.

"You!" The one with the handle-bar mustache stabbed a finger at Rocca. "You, greaser. They tell me you are a friend of the man named Battles."

Rocca was like a coiled snake. He looked at them, and he smiled. Now no Mex likes to be called a greaser. Me, I've been called a gringo many times and couldn't see that it left any scars, but some folks are almighty touchy, and Rocca was that way now. Not that I blamed him. It is all very easy to say trouble can be avoided, but these men were not going to be avoided. They were looking for trouble; they wanted it.

"Si, *señor*," Rocca said gently, "I am honored to call John J. Battles my friend."

"Then I guess we'll just kill you, Mex, seein' as how we can't find him."

Well, I just looked up at the man and I said, "I'm a friend of his, too," and I said it sort of off-hand as if it didn't matter much, but they knew it did.

They turned their eyes on me, and I just sat there, a tall, lonely man in a wore-out buckskin shirt and a beat-up hat.

"You want part of this?" Walrus-mustache was speaking again.

"A man can ride many a long mile in Texas," I said, "and see nothing but grass and sky. There's streams down there, and a man could raise some cows. Here in

Arizona there's timber country with fine, beautiful meadows and cold mountain streams—"

"What're you talkin' about?" Handle-bar mustache broke in. "Are you crazy?"

"I was just thinking a man would have to be an awful fool to throw all that away to prove how mean he was. I mean you boys got a choice. You walk back over there and drink your liquor and ride out to those mountain streams where the tall grass grows."

"Or—?"

"Or you stay here, and tomorrow you'll be pushin' grass from the under side."

They stared at me. They were trying to figure whether I was all talk, or whether I was tough. Now, I'm a patient man. Had they been talking to Tyrel, folks would have been laying out the bodies by now. Me, I'm not backward about giving a man a chance. Many a time a man with whiskey in him is apt to talk too much, and suddenly realize he wished he was somewhere else. I was giving them this chance.

They didn't take it.

The long-geared man with the handle-bar mustache looked at me and said, "I'm Arch Hadden," as if he expected me to show scare at the name.

"Glad to meet you, Mr. Hadden," I said gently. "I'll carve the slab myself."

He kind of flushed up, and I could see he was off his step, somehow. He'd come walking up to fight, and my talk had put him off. Also, that name meant nothing to me, and I never was one to put much stock in reputations, anyway.

Rocca had let me talk; he just sat quiet, but I'd come up the trail from Yuma with Tampico Rocca, and knew he was no man to buy trouble with. Arch Hadden had lost step, and he tried to get back again.

"I came to kill this greaser, an' I aim to do it."

Rocca came to his feet in one smooth, easy movement. "Then why not get started?"

The man with the walrus mustache had had more to drink, and he wasn't being bluffed. He went for his gun, and I straightened my leg with a snap. The chair slammed into his legs and he fell against Hadden, and I shot the man on the end while they were falling. I heard another gun boom and then Rocca and me were standing there looking down at Hadden and his brother, one of them in a half-crouch but off balance, the other on one knee.

"You boys brought it to us," I said. "We didn't ask for it. You brought it, and now two of you are dead."

They hadn't looked at their companions until then, and when they did I saw they were suddenly cold sober.

"Arch," I said, "you may be a tough man where you come from, but you're a long way from home. You take my advice and go back.

Rocca was holding a gun on them, as I was. He reached around with his other hand and picked up his beer, and drank it, watching them.

Foster was standing across the room, his back to the bar. "Why don't you boys pack it up before the law gets here?" he suggested. "I don't want any more shooting in here. It's bad for business."

"Sure," I said, and holstered my gun. Deliberately I started for the door.

Tampico Rocca had been called a greaser, so he took his time. He put his glass down gently and he smiled at them. "Keep your guns," he said, "I want to meet you again, *señores*."

Outside in the street we ducked into an alley and stood listening for footsteps, but hearing none, we walked away.

At the corral we stopped and leaned on the bars, and Rocca built a cigarette. *"Gracias, amigo,"* he said. And then he added, "You are quick, *amigo*. You are very quick."

Chapter 4

COME DAYBREAK, and worry was upon me. It was a real, old-fashioned attack of the dismals.

The shooting of the night before was bad enough, although I never gave much time to worry over those who came asking for trouble. When a man packed a gun he was supposed to give some thought to his actions and his manner of speech, for folks weren't much inclined to set back and let a body run over them.

It was that youngster who was worrying me. There was a small boy, a prisoner of the Apaches, or maybe already killed by them. And he was my blood kin.

Nobody knew better than me the distance I'd have to cover and the way I'd have to live for the next month or more. It was a hard country, almost empty of people, scarce of food, and rare of water that was fit to drink.

The fact that Tampico Rocca was coming along sort of made it better. Two men can't move as quiet as one, except when one of them is Rocca. But his coming also made it worse, because if anything happened to him it would be because of me.

Now the first thing I needed was a horse, and I could find none for sale. Meantime I sort of sauntered around and let folks know I needed a saddle, and finally bought a beat-up old Spanish single-rig saddle with a *mochila*, or housing, to throw over it, and oxbow stirrups. It was almighty old, but in good shape, and a lot of hard use had worn comfort into it. That saddle set me back eighteen dollars, and I picked up some old saddlebags for

32

three dollars more. An old Army canteen cost me
twenty-five cents. Little by little I put an outfit together,
and by the time I'd bought a spare cartridge belt, a
bridle, and a few other odds and ends I'd spent more
than fifty dollars of what little I had. And still no horse.

Whilst I went around the town of Tucson I kept a
careful eye open for Arch and Wolf Hadden. It turned
out that one of those boys shot the night before wasn't
dead. He'd been hit hard, but he was going to pull
through. They planted the other one, wrapped in his
blankets, out on Boot Hill.

By noontime I had most of what I would need, but
was still shy a horse. Dropping in at the Shoo-Fly I
figured to have myself a bite of grub, and maybe I could
find somebody with a horse to spare.

So I shaved myself with a broken triangle of glass for
a mirror, stuck in the fork of a mesquite tree, while
Rocca slept with his head on his saddle close by. We
were a mite out of town among some rocks and mesquite, and we'd been there a while when I heard somebody singing "Oh, Bury Me Not on the Lone Prairee,"
and Rocca pushed his hat back off his eyes. "Don't
shoot," he said, grinning at me. "That's John J."

And it was. Battles came up through the brush and
looked us over, and we told him what the score was.

"Where's Spanish?" he wanted to know, and Rocca
told him.

"He found himself a gal down yonder. Her name is
Conchita, and if she gets mad at him the Apaches will
be a relief. But don't you worry none about Spanish.
When the time comes he'll fork his saddle and come
with us."

When I'd shaved we talked things over a mite and
Rocca headed for Mexican town to roust out Spanish
Murphy, whilst Battles went back into the brush to keep
out of sight. Somehow or other, neither of us thought to
tell him about the Hadden outfit.

The Shoo-Fly was crowded when I came in, but I
turned some heads. I don't know if it was the gun battle
the night before or the whiskey I'd used for shave lotion,

but they looked me over some. I'd been sort of side-
stepping the marshal, not wanting to be ordered out of
town yet, and not wanting trouble, if he was so inclined.

When it came to eating, I was always a good feeder
and always ready to set up and partake. Likely this
would be the last woman-cooked food I'd have for a
while, and even any hot meals I'd cook myself would
be almighty scarce on that trek down into Sonora and
over into Chihuahua. When a man is fighting shy of
Apaches he doesn't go around sending up smoke.

Sitting there in the Shoo-Fly, which was not exactly
elegant, though the best there was around, a body might
have an idea folks would step aside for a body who'd
killed his man in a gun battle. No such thing.

Right there in that room there were men like William
S. Oury, who had fought through the Texas war for
independence, had been a Texas Ranger, and had engaged in many a bloody duel with Apaches and border
characters. Most of the men sitting around in their
broadcloth suits were men who had engaged in their
share of Indian fights, or wars of one kind or another.
And they were good citizens—lawyers, mining men,
storekeepers and the like.

No sooner had I begun to eat than the door opened
and Laura came in. She was in white, and she looked
pale and frail. She wore the kind of gloves with no fingers in them that made no sense to me. And she carried
a parasol, as most women did.

She stood a moment, letting her eyes grow accustomed to the glare, and then crossed to my table. I got
up and seated her, then sat down.

Folks turned to look at her; they were almighty
curious, her being such a pretty woman and all, and not
many of them knowing we were kin.

"Tell," she said, "I heard you were looking for a
horse. Is that true?"

"Yes, ma'am, it is. Mine was killed out yonder. I've
got to find a saddle horse and at least one pack horse.
Seems Apache raids have cut down the supply, and the
Army has been buying saddle stock, too."

"Why didn't you tell me? I can get you some horses. In fact, I have just the horse for you."

"It would help," I admitted. "I've got my outfit together."

She took the coffee Mrs. Wallen brought to the table, and then said, "I hear you had some trouble."

"It wasn't my trouble. They were hunting a man I know, and when they couldn't find him they chose me—that is, me and Rocca, one of the men I rode to town with."

She said no more about it, and I wasn't anxious to talk of it. We talked a while about the trip, and then she told me where to go to see the horses. "The one I want you to ride," she suggested, "is the big black with the diamond blaze on his hip."

Now, one horse I was not hunting was a big black with a diamond on his hip. Any kind of horse would help, but a black horse was almost as bad as a white one in that country. What I preferred was a roan, a buckskin, or a dun or *grulla*. I wanted a horse whose color would fade into the country, not one that would stand out like a red nose at a teetotal picnic. Of course, there were patches of black rock, shadows, and the like, and a black horse was some better than a white one which would catch the sun and could be seen for miles. However, this was no time to argue.

"All right," I said; and then I added, "If we get the horses I can leave tomorrow."

She talked of Tucson and its discomforts, and how she wished to be back in Santa Fe—or in Washington, she added.

"I like Washington," I said.

She seemed surprised, and said, "You have been there?"

"Yes, ma'am. I was in the Army of the Potomac for a while. I was around Washington quite a bit."

That was a long time ago, and I'd been a boy then, freshly joined up with the Union army.

When she was gone I lingered over coffee, thinking out that trail to the south, trying to foresee the problems that might arise. It wasn't in me to go into things blind, and there was a whole lot about this that made me kind of uneasy, but there was nothing I could pin down.

Mrs. Wallen came over. "Are you related to Laura Sackett?"

"She's my sister-in-law."

"I wondered . . . your names being the same, and all." She still hesitated, then sat down opposite me. "We don't see many women traveling alone in this country."

"Her father died . . . out in Californy," I said. "He was all alone out there, and nobody to see to him. Orrin —he's my brother—had to stay in Washington."

She sat there a while without saying any more, and then got up and left. I couldn't figure out why she sat down to talk to me. It seemed as if she was going to tell me something—maybe something about the Army or the Apaches.

The black horse was a good one, all right. And that diamond-shaped blaze on his hip and one white stocking was all that kept him from being solid black. He was a whole lot more horse than I expected to find. The two pack horses were nondescript mustangs, but they looked tough.

They were in a barn back of an adobe, and the man who had the care of them squatted on his heels and watched me studying the horses.

"You're takin' a lot of care, mister," he said sourly, "when you got no choice."

He spat out the straw he'd been chewing. "Take 'em or leave 'em. I got no more time to spare. The lady paid for 'em. All you got to do is saddle up and ride."

He didn't like me and I didn't like him, so I taken the horses and got away. I rode them back into the brush where Rocca was waiting and where my gear was cached.

Rocca had rustled a horse from somewhere in Mex town, so we were ready to go.

"You got anything holdin' you?" I asked him.

"Not so's you'd notice. Spanish is out in the brush with John J. They'll meet us south of here."

So we mounted up and rode out of there, paying no mind to anything else. Down country about four miles Spanish rode up to us, and then John J. Battles followed.

"You boys are taking a wild chance," I said. "You got no stake in this."

"Shut up," Spanish said. "You save your breath to cool your porridge."

"I never been to the Sierra Madres," John J. said. "Any place I ain't been I got to see."

We put up some dust and headed south, with me riding up front. The trail was used . . . there was always some riding down toward Kitchen's ranch.

You might think that on a traveled trail you'd be safe, but there was nowhere in this corner of Arizona where a body was safe, one moment to the next. Pete Kitchen had men on watch all hours of the day, and everybody went armed, expecting trouble, so after a while the Apaches kind of fought shy of the Kitchen outfit.

There's been a lot of talk of the rights and wrongs of the Indian wars, and there was wrong on both sides. There were mighty few Indians holding down land in this country when the white man came, and most of them never held to any one spot. They just drifted from place to place, living off the wild game and the plants. The white men came hunting living space, and a place for a home. Instead of roaming as the Indians had done, they settled down to farm the land and build houses.

Some of the white men wanted to live in peace with the red man, and some of the red men wanted to live in peace, too; but some on both sides didn't want anything of the kind. The young bucks wanted to take scalps and steal horses because that made them big men with the squaws, and it was often easier to take them from white men than from other Indians, as they had always done. And whenever the wise old Indians and the wiser and kinder of the white men wanted to make peace, there was always some drunken white man or wild-haired Indian ready to make trouble.

When an Indian made war he made war on women and children as well as on men, and even the friendly white men found it hard to be friendly when they came home and found their cabins burned, their women and children killed. On the other hand, the politically appointed Indian agents and the white men who wanted Indian land or horses would rob, cheat, and murder Indians.

It was no one-sided argument, and I knew it. But now the Apaches had stolen some children and taken them into Mexico, and we were going after them.

We rode through the last of the afternoon and into the cool of the evening. We camped that night in some ruins, half sheltered by adobe walls, and at daybreak we rode out.

On the second night we stayed at Pete Kitchen's ranch.

Chapter 5

WE RODE SOUTH for a few miles after leaving Pete Kitchen's place, then turned off the main trail toward the east. Now, a man who leaves a trail in the desert had best know exactly where he is going, for his life is at stake.

Travel in the desert cannot be haphazard. Every step a man takes in desert country has to be taken with water in mind. He is either heading for water, or figuring how far he will be from it if he gets off the trail. The margin of safety is narrow.

All of us had been south of the border, but it was Tampico Rocca who knew most about it, with me coming second, I suppose. Like everybody else, we had to depend on waterholes, and no matter what route we chose, sooner or later we had to wind up at those watering places. This was just as true for the Apaches.

The desert has known waterholes, but it also has other waterholes not generally known, usually of limited capacity and usually difficult to find. Birds and animals know of those places, and so do the Apaches in most cases. If you did not know of them you had to know how to find them, and that was something that did not come easy.

A man living in wild country has to be aware of everything around him. He has to keep his eyes looking, his ears listening, his every sense alert. And that doesn't mean because of Apaches, but because of the desert itself. You can't fight the desert . . . you have to ride with it.

The desert is not all hot sun and sand; there's the rocks too. Miles of them sometimes, scattered over the desert floor, great heaps of them now and again, or those great broken ridges of dull red or black rock like the broken spines of huge animals. They shove up through the sand, and the sand is trying hard to bury them again.

In much of the southwestern desert there's even a lot of green, although the *playas,* or dry lake beds, are dead white. Some of the desert plants hold back until there's a rain, then they leaf out suddenly and blossom quickly, to take advantage of that water. But much of the greenness of desert plants doesn't mean that rain has fallen, for many of the plants have stored water in their pulpy tissues to save against drought; others have developed hard-surfaced leaves that reflect sunlight and give off no moisture to the sun.

Plants and animals have learned to live with the desert, and so have the Apaches. And we, the four of us, we were like Apaches in that regard.

The desert is the enemy of the careless. Neither time, nor trails, nor equipment will ever change that. A man must stay alert to choose the easiest routes, he travels slow to save himself, he keeps his eyes open to see those signs which indicate where water might be found. The flight of bees or birds, the tracks of small animals, the kind of plants he sees—these things he must notice, for certain plants are indications of ground water, and some birds and animals never live far from water. Others drink little, or rarely, getting the moisture they need from the plants they eat or the animals they kill.

We rode until the sun was two hours in the sky, and then we turned off into a narrow canyon and hunted shade to wait through the hottest hours. We unsaddled, let the horses roll, then watered them at a little seep Rocca knew of. After that, with one man to watch, we stretched out on the sand to catch some rest.

There always had to be a man on watch, because the

Apaches were great horse thieves, though not a patch on the Comanches, who could steal a horse from under you whilst you sat in the saddle. You either kept watch or you found yourself afoot; and in the desert, unless you're almighty canny, that means you're dead.

First off, when we rode into that canyon we studied the opening for sign. A man in wild country soon gets so he can read the trail sign as easy as most folks read a newspaper, and often it's even more interesting.

You not only read what sign you see on the ground, but you learn to read dust in the distant air—how many riders there are under that dust, and where they're headed.

The droppings left by horses also have a story to tell; whether that horse has been grain-fed, whether he has been grazing off country grass or desert plants.

And no two horses leave the same track. Each is a mite different, and their gaits are different. Their hoofs do not strike with the same impact, and sometimes there's a difference in the way they are shod.

We could tell that nobody had been in that canyon for weeks. We knew, too, that most of the time during the months of June, July, and August in Sonora you'll get some rain. Sudden showers that may be gone as quickly as they come, but enough to settle the dust and to fill some of the "tanks" in the desert mountains.

Among those desert ridges such tanks are frequent, pits hollowed in the rock over the centuries by driving rain, or shaped by run-off water. During heavy rains these tanks collect water and hold it for weeks, or even for months. We'd had some rain, so the better water-holes and tanks were holding water now.

Shortly before sundown, rested by our nap in the shade, we saddled up again. This time I taken the lead.

There were clusters of *cholla* and *ocotillo,* and we took advantage of them as much as possible to shield our movements. The route we used was an ancient one rarely traveled in these days, but from time to time we'd pull up near a clump of brush where the outlines of our horses and ourselves would merge into the growth, and there we'd set, studying the country around us.

You might think that out in such open country, with no good cover anywhere, a body wouldn't have to worry, but knowing Apaches the way we did, we knew that twenty of them could be hidden out there in a matter of yards, and nobody the wiser.

We were taking our time, saving our horses. An Apache, who often rode his horses to death, will make sixty to seventy miles a day if he's in a hurry. On foot he'll cover thirty-five to forty miles a day even in rough country. That was about what we were doing a-horseback.

About an hour after dark we rode down into a little hollow choked with mesquite brush and built ourselves a tiny fire of dried wood and made coffee. The fire was well hidden in the hollow and the brush, and it gave us a chance to get the coffee we dearly needed.

"What you think?" Rocca said suddenly. "One rider?"

"Uh-huh," I said; "a small man or a boy."

"What are you talking about?" Battles asked.

"We've been picking up tracks," I told them. "A shod horse. A small horse, but a good one. Moves well . . . desert bred."

"Injun, on a stolen horse," Spanish said promptly. "No white man would be ridin' alone in this neck of the woods."

Rocca shrugged doubtfully. "Maybe so . . . I don't know."

Those tracks had been worrying my mind for quite a few minutes, for whoever rode that horse was riding with caution, which meant it was no Apache. An Apache would know he was in country where his people were supreme; and although he would keep alert, he would not be pausing to scout the country as this rider was.

In my mind I was sure, and I knew Rocca was sure, that the rider was no Indian. Unless, maybe, an Indian child.

When the desert sun was gone the heat went with it, and a coolness came over the land. The horses, quickened by the cool air, moved forward as eagerly as if they could already smell the pines of the Sierra Madre. From time to time we drew up to listen into the night.

About an hour before daylight we gave our horses a breather. Rocca, squatting on his heels behind a mesquite bush, lit a cigarette cupped in the palm of his hand and glanced at me. "You know the Bavispe?"

"Yes . . . we'll hit at the big bend . . . where she turns south again."

Tampico Rocca knew this country better than I did. After all, he was half Apache, and he had lived in the Sierra Madre. Battles was sleeping, and Spanish he went over to listen to the night sounds, away from our voices. I was hot and tired, and was wishing for a bath in that river up ahead, but it wasn't likely I'd get one.

Rocca was quiet for a spell, and I settled back on the sand and stared up at the stars. They looked lonely up there in the nighttime sky, lonely as we were down here. I was a solitary man, a drifter across the country, with no more home than a tumbleweed, but so were we all. We were men without women, and if all the nights we'd spent under a roof were put together they would scarcely cover four or five weeks.

Men have a way of drifting together without much rhyme or reason; just the circumstances of their living brings them together, just as we had been brought together in Yuma. Now the three of them were chancing their lives to lend me a hand; but that was the way with western men, and chances were I'd have done the same for them.

We started on again when the first streaks of dawn were coloring the eastern sky. The cactus began to be separate from the other shadows, and the rocks stood out, dark and somber. We rode single file, nobody talking until the gray sky was yellowing overhead, and then in a quiet corner we stopped, found a place to hide a fire, and made a small breakfast.

We were careful to build our fire in a hollow and under a mesquite bush, where the rising smoke would be dissipated by the branches overhead . . . though using dry wood there was little smoke. Our time for hot meals was about over. Barring some sort of accident, we should soon come up to the Bavispe. Once we crossed that we would be in the heart of Apache country, with them on every side of us.

The Apache, in a sparse, harsh land where raising any crops was mighty nigh impossible, turned to raiding and robbing.

Generally, the men I'd heard talk of the Indian thought it was taking his land that ruined him. As a matter of fact, it had much to do with it, for an Indian couldn't live on a fixed ten acres or a hundred acres and live as he liked. He needed lots of hunting ground, and country that would support fifty Indians would support ten thousand planting white men.

But the Indian was whipped the first time one of them had a rifle for his own. It was the trader who whipped the Indian by giving or selling him things he couldn't make himself. From that time on, the Indian was dependent on the white man for ammunition, for more guns, for more of the things he was getting a taste for.

It was good sitting there in the cool of early morning, with the faint smell of woodsmoke in the air, the smell of frying bacon, the smell of good coffee. We were taking a chance, but we had scouted the country with care.

"How old's the boy?" Spanish asked suddenly.

"Five . . . I think. About that."

"You think he's still alive, Tamp?" Battles asked.

Rocca shrugged. "Depends on whether he's a nervy kid, maybe. We'll pick up some tracks soon."

"Seen any more of that strange rider?" Battles asked. "I been watching for tracks all morning."

"No," I said, "I haven't seen any."

"What's it like up yonder?" Spanish asked.

"Oaks . . . then pines. Running streams, rocks. All anybody could want but grub. They have to bring it in. They get it from the Mexicans, or they kill them." He gestured. "The Apaches have almost cleared this part of

Sonora of the Mexicans. At least the rich ones. And the poor ones can only stay if they'll provide food for the Apaches."

My thoughts went back over the desert to Laura. She was a pretty woman, and she was brave . . . holding herself up, like she did, with her little boy lost, and all. But somehow she left me uneasy. But I was never very comfortable around women . . . except Ange. And the Trelawney girls I'd known back home in the hills.

We sat there quiet a little longer, listening to the horses cropping at the shrubs. Rocca was smoking and squinting at the hills around.

None of us knew what might be waiting for us up yonder. Even if we found the boy alive, we still had to get him from the Apaches and get him back across the border. Our chances were none too good. I looked over at Rocca and said, "Shall we move out?"

He rubbed his cigarette into the sand, and got up.

Me, I just stood there a moment or two thinking. All of a sudden I wished I was somewhere else. We were facing up to a lot of hell, and I looked forward to none of it. Besides, there was something about this whole affair that made me mighty uneasy.

We crossed the Bavispe and took a thin trail that led up through scattered oaks, along steep switchbacks toward the pines. The only sound was the chirping of birds, the grunting of one of the horses over a steep part of the trail, or the clatter of a falling rock.

For an hour we climbed, pausing several times to let the horses catch their breath. Finally we rode out on a bench under the pines where stood the ruins of stone houses built of rough lava blocks with no mortar. There were at least a dozen of them in sight, and maybe more back under the trees. The walls were of a sort of gray felsite, and here and there one appeared to be better built than the others, as though built by different hands, by different thinking.

Rocca indicated a slight depression in the grass near one of the walls. "We're still on the trail."

A crushed pine cone looked as if it had been scarred by a sharp-shod hoof. There were other signs too.

The country here was wild and rugged, and we saw no water. We were now over six thousand feet up, judging by the growth around us, and still we climbed. The trail occasionally wound along a rim with an almost sheer drop falling off on one side or the other. We rode with our rifles in our hands, our boots light in the stirrups, ready to kick free and hit the ground if there was time. Riding that kind of country with Apaches around will put gray in your hair.

We came out presently on a shoulder of the mountain with pines all around us. There was sparse grass, and a thin trickle of snow water ran down the mountain slope. Found the tracks of the rider there . . . plain. The small horse had stood under a tree, tied to a low branch while she scouted ahead.

She?

The word came to me unbidden, without thinking. It came like a voice speaking to me, and I spoke aloud what I had heard in my mind's ear. "It's a woman, Tamp. That's a woman or girl riding that horse."

Rocca rested his big hands on the pommel. "I think you are right," he said. "I think so."

"A woman?" Battles was incredulous. "It don't stand to reason."

"Did Dan Creed have a wife? Or a daughter?" I asked.

Rocca looked around at me. "I don' know, Tell. I tell you, I don'."

I dropped to the ground. "Sit tight," I said. "I want to see what she went to look at."

A step or two and it was dark and green under the trees. A step or two more and I was lost to them, waiting back there for me. I could see a pressed-down leaf here, and the kicked-over damp, dead leaves, scuffed by a passing boot. The trail was easy, but it took time, for I scouted the trees around me as I moved.

Suddenly—a running man could scarcely have stopped in time—I was on the brink of a cliff. Not sheer, but a steep falling away, something a man could climb down if he could find foothold and used his hands, or if he could slide.

It was maybe a couple of thousand feet down to the bottom, and there was a meadow, the greenest you ever saw, and a pool with trees around it. It was a small hanging valley that opened out over an enormous canyon. There were three cooking fires in sight, and a dozen Apaches.

First I squatted down, easing down so my movement would draw no attention, and then I studied the camp through a manzanita growing on the rim.

Squaws were working, children playing. They felt secure here. Nobody had ever followed them into this country; nobody had ever found them here before. For years, for generations, they had been coming here after their raids, after stealing the cattle, the horses, and the women of the Mexicans. Stealing their food, too, and bringing it here and to other places like this . . . there must be many of them.

Little Orry was in one of them. How long could we look before they caught us?

How long, then, could we expect to live?

But Orry was my brother's son, and I was a Sackett, and in the Sackett veins the blood ran strong and true. It was our nature and our upbringing.

A few minutes longer I squatted there, watching the camp. Not staring, for staring can be felt, and will make an animal or an Indian uneasy. Then I went back through the trees.

"It's a *rancheria*," I said, "but I doubt if it is the one we want."

Chapter 6

WHOEVER IT WAS who had come up the mountain before us had spent a good bit of time studying that camp. There were a-plenty of tracks, knee impressions, and the like, so we could see whoever it was had stayed there quite some time. And then that person had mounted up and ridden on.

We, too, moved on, and the trail we now followed was a deer trail . . . or maybe one made by big horn sheep, which leave a somewhat similar track. The only other tracks on the trail were those small hoof prints, or sometimes, when the rider got off and walked, were boot tracks.

We entered soon into a wild and broken country, past towering masses of conglomerate and streams of a dull opalescent water, slightly bitter to the taste, but nonetheless good for drinking. Many times we were forced to dismount and lead our mounts, for large limbs or out-thrusts of rock projected over the trail.

Among some pines we pulled off and got down from our saddles. Tampico Rocca hunkered down and stared at the ground. Spanish Murphy glanced over at me. "Tell . . . you think we're going to find that boy?"

"Uh-huh."

Well, I knew what he was feeling. The quiet. It was getting us. We were in the heart of Indian country, and we were all jumpy. There wasn't one of us who didn't know what it would mean if we were seen. It would mean a running fight . . .and our only choice would be to try to get away.

Once it was known we were around we'd have no chance to get close to those children. So far we'd had luck, with the skill of Rocca to provide a good part of it —his skill and his knowledge of the country.

Presently we moved on, and now we saw Indian tracks from time to time. Up to now we had been traveling high, lonely country where Indians seldom went, but now we were descending slowly, getting into the areas where there was game, and where at any time we might encounter Indians.

"There's another *rancheria* ahead," Rocca soon said.

This one was also in a hollow, with a towering cliff behind it, and low, rolling pine-clad hills around. The *rancheria* lay in a nest of boulders and trees, with a small stream curving around the encampment. Even as we came up through the pines, several horsemen arrived. They rode into the area accompanied by a small swirl of dust and dropped to the ground. There were six Apaches in the group, four of them armed with bows, two with rifles.

Two of them were carrying chunks of meat, probably from slaughtered cattle. A third was handing down some articles of clothing, evidently stripped from some Mexican or his wife—from our distance we could not determine which.

Suddenly Battles grabbed my arm and pointed. Several children had come up, carrying bundles of sticks. At least one appeared to be a white boy; his face was partly turned from them. He was a tall youngster, perhaps eight or nine years old.

This could be the place. Whatever else we did, we must talk to that boy.

I was conscious of the fresh smell of the pines and of crushed pine needles underfoot. There was a faint smell of smoke from the camp, and I could make out the sound of Indian voices speaking. Inside me, I was still—waiting, thinking.

If there were other white children around, that boy

would know about them. But what if he had already become close to being an Apache? Taken young enough, many American or Mexican children had no wish to leave the Apaches. To speak to him was a risk, but it must be done.

Spanish, he looked over at me. "We got us a job, boy," he said.

"I never figured it to be easy." I studied the *rancheria,* and I did not feel happy about the situation.

"We're too close," Rocca said. "We'd better move back. If the wind changed a mite, the dogs could smell us."

So we moved back among the trees and, weaving around a little, we found ourselves a tree-shaded hollow with a lot of boulders around and some big trees. It was a perfect place to hide, and we were out of the wind there.

But I was worried. When I traveled alone, as I most often did, I had nobody to worry about but myself, and if I got into trouble there was only my own scalp to lose. This shape-up was entirely different, for these men had come along only to help me. If anything happened to them I'd have it on my mind.

We were here, though, and we had a job to do. "Rocca," I said, "is it likely that boy yonder would ever be left alone?"

"I doubt it. Depend on how long he's been with them, and how much they've come to trust him. There's a chance maybe."

"He'd be likely to know about other white youngsters, wouldn't he?"

"It's likely. Word gets around, and the Apache children would know, and they'd be apt to speak of it. At least when I was a boy in those Apache camps I knew most of what went on."

For the time being there was nothing much we could do, so the others stretched out to catch a little sleep, and I worked up to the bluff to get a better look than we'd had before.

The camp was quiet. The squaws never stopped working, of course, always busy at something, and a few youngsters played around. One of the Apache braves we had seen ride into camp sat cross-legged in front of his wickiup. He was a stoop-shouldered but strongly made man of about my own age, and he had a new Winchester that was never far from his hand. Even here, in their own hide-out, they never let up.

After a while I returned to camp and Spanish took my place up on the bluff. Under a low tree I settled down for some rest.

When I awoke I fought myself back to reality with an effort. I'd been dog-tired, and whilst I usually was ready to wake up on the slightest sound, this time I had really slept.

The first thing I noticed was the silence. There was no fire, of course, and there was little light. It was late afternoon, and under the trees it was already shading down to dusk.

For a moment I lay quiet, listening. Raising my head, I looked around. Over yonder there was a saddle—I could see the faint shine of it. I could see nothing else, nor could I hear any sound but the soft rustling of the leaves overhead.

My right hand moved for my rifle, closed around the action. A shot fired here would bring Apaches around us like bees from a kicked hive.

Carefully, I eased back the blanket, moved my feet out, and then drew them up and rolled to my knees. Glancing to where John J. Battles was lying, I could see his body under a blanket. He was asleep . . . at least he was not moving.

Rocca was nowhere in sight; his bed was empty. We had purposely scattered out to sleep. It gave us that much more of a chance if the camp was attacked.

A moment longer I waited, then came up swiftly and with one long step was molded into the shadow of a tree. And still nothing stirred.

Nevertheless, I knew it wasn't just a case of worry with me. Somebody or something was prowling our camp, and we were too close to those Apaches for comfort. At the same time I know that the Apache, generally speaking, won't fight after dark. He has the feeling that the soul of a man killed in the night wanders forever in darkness.

Of a sudden, something moved near me.

There was no light but that of the stars. Here and there a tree trunk stood out, or a leaf caught the shine of a reflection.

It was a haunted place, this camp of ours, a corner among the crags, a place where cliffs reared up or fell away, where broken rocks lay among the trees. There were so many shadows that one saw nothing clearly.

Slowly I lowered the butt of my rifle to the ground. At my belt was a bowie knife, sharp enough to shave with—in fact, I often did shave with it. But it was my hands on which I would depend this time; hard work had made them strong, had built muscles into my arms and shoulders. For little softness had come into my life, little but hard riding and harder work. I waited, my hands ready.

The movement was there again, not a sound so much as a suggestion. Then it was the breathing that warned me . . . only breathing, and I reached out with my hands.

Something slipped through my hands like a ghost. My hands touched it, grasped, and the thing wasn't there . . . a faint grasp, and my fingers clutched only hair . . . then it was gone!

Battles sat up. "Tell? What is it?"

"A ghost, I think." I spoke softly. "Whatever it is, I wish it would believe we're not enemies."

But whatever it was, was gone.

A couple of hours later, by the light of day, we found tracks enough. Tip toe tracks of a small foot. I felt a shudder go through me, and Rocca noticed it. "What?" he said. "You are afraid?"

"I was remembering . . . someone who is gone," I said. "But these tracks are not hers. They are small, like hers, and the steps are quick, like hers . . . but she is dead."

Tampico Rocca crossed himself. "She haunts you?"

"No . . . it is only a memory. Her name was Ange, and I found her trail first, like this. I lost her again, like this. But Ange is dead. She was murdered," I said, "up in the Mogollon country."

"Ah!" That was Spanish. "You are *that* Sackett!" He looked at me thoughtfully. "I heard talk of it. I was in Cherry Creek then, but everybody knew the story . . . and how your family came to help."

He looked at me over the tip of his cigarette, and I could guess what he was thinking. In the western lands where all news came by word of mouth, men quickly became legend, they became larger than life. It was so with Ben Thompson, Wild Bill, Mike Fink, or Davy Crockett. The stories grew with telling.

"The boy we're hunting," I said, "is my brother Orrin's boy. Orrin was one of them who rode to the Mogollon."

"I never had a family," Spanish said. "I was always alone."

John J. tamped tobacco into his pipe. "Most men are alone," he said. "We come into life alone, we face our worst troubles alone, and we are alone when we die."

"It was the girl we tracked," I said. I'd been looking around while we talked. "She needed grub. She's taken some bread and some dried apples, and maybe a little jerky."

And then we were quiet again.

We knew what we had to do, and the waiting was hard, for we were men who preferred action. Our way of life had been to act . . . there was rarely need for contemplation. We were men who moved swiftly, surely, and we lived or died by the success of our movement. So to wait now came hard. To wander in the mountains added to our danger, and to wait here was risk, but a man who does not move leaves no tracks.

So we watched and waited, for it was all we could do, and even just watching worried me for men who are being watched become aware of it.

The white boy we had seen appeared again, more

than once, but always with Indian boys around him.
And then, after another long day of watching, I saw him
take a spear and go alone along a trail between some
rocks. Like a cat I was off the rock where I watched,
nodding to Rocca as I passed him.

Spanish went up to watch from where I had been,
and John J. went to the horses—we saddled them each
morning—to be ready in case of need.

Tampico Rocca was a ghost on the trail, moving
without sound. We snaked down among the rocks,
crawled over great boulders, and came down to where
we could await the boy.

Was he changed? Had he become an Apache? If so,
he would shout when he saw us.

Only he had no chance. Soundlessly Rocca dropped
to the trail behind him, put one hand over the boy's
mouth, and lifted him into the brush, where we
crouched.

He looked wild-eyed with fright, then seeing we were
white men he tried to speak. Slowly Rocca took his hand
from his mouth.

"Take me away!" he whispered. "My name is Brook.
Harry Brook."

"How long have they had you?"

"Two years, I think. Maybe not that long, but a long
time."

"Where are the other white children? The Creeds and
Orry Sackett."

"The Creeds? I have heard of them. They are in the
next *rancheria*." He pointed. "Over there."

"And the Sackett boy?"

"I do not know. I never heard of another boy. There
is a girl with the Creed boys, but she is only five . . .
very small."

Well . . . something seemed to drain away inside me.
Had they killed him then? Had they killed Orrin's son?

Battles asked the question.

"Nobody was killed," the boys said. "I was in camp
when they brought them in, the Creed boys and the
girl."

Squatting down on my heels, I asked, "Can you get to those others? I mean, will you ever see them?"

"You ain't takin' me along with you?" There were tears in his eyes.

"Not right now. Look, if we took you now we'd have to run, wouldn't we? All right, we leave you here. You be ready." I pointed toward a high rock. "Can you see that from camp?"

"Yes."

"All right . . . when you see a black rock atop that, you come to this place, right here. We've got to get those other youngsters."

"You'll get killed. They're in Kahtenny's *rancheria.*"

"Kahtenny? He's alive, then?"

"He sure is. An' all them Apaches yonder take a back seat for him. He's a big man among 'em."

We left him then, worried for fear the Apaches would come scouting to see what he was doing. They trusted no prisoner, even if he seemed to accept their ways. Only thing was, they didn't figure anybody could get away from the Sierra Madres . . . or that anybody would dare come in after them.

The first thing I did was hunt a piece of black lava rock to use when the time came. I placed it handy under a bush, and we went back, mounted up, and followed a trail out of there, skirting a cliff that fell away so sharply you felt as if you rode on a piece of molding along a wall.

That boy back there . . . could he keep them from knowing? That troubled me some.

There was small chance he could get to the other youngsters, but there was some visiting back and forth . . . it could be.

But where was Orry Sackett? Where was my brother's son?

Chapter 7

THROUGH THE CHILL DAWN we climbed toward the high peaks, weaving our way among trees that dripped with moisture from the low-hanging clouds. Then we descended several hundred feet into a secluded park ringed with splendid pines. On the far side a cold, clear stream fell over a limestone ledge into a deep pool.

In every sheltered spot there were ruins . . . ancient ruins, half buried in earth or an overgrowth of brush or moss. In one place a gnarled and twisted cedar grew inside a wall, a cedar that itself must have been hundreds of years old.

I questioned Rocca, and he shrugged. "Who knows? They were the People Who Came Before, and they were gone before the Apaches came."

He was only mildly curious. "Many peoples have come and gone. It is the way of the world. The People of the Stone Houses . . . the people who built the cliff dwellings in Arizona and Colorado. They were driven out by the Navajo, who killed many of them.

"The white man has driven out the Indian, but the Indian drove out others before, and those others had driven peoples before them. It is always the same. I think the Indian was defeated by the traders, not by the soldiers."

"How so?" Battles asked.

"The traders made the Indian want things he could not make himself. He came to need the white man, to depend upon him. The Indian had to trade or steal to get the rifles and other things he wanted that the white man had."

It was what I had thought myself.

Rocca shrugged again. "The first white trader who came to the Indians brought their doom in his pack. I think it is so."

We were silent then. We came to a fearful slide and went down it, our horses sliding on their haunches for a good part of the distance to the bottom of a gloomy canyon, through which ran the headwaters of the Bavispe. It was an eerie, haunted spot, and I swung down, standing for a moment with both hands on the saddle, listening. But there was no sound except that of falling water, and the sighing of wind among the pines.

"I don't like it," John J. said. "It looks like the dark edge of hell."

Me, I was thinking of those youngsters among the Apaches, so strange to them, so frightening. They must be scared stiff. Yet I could think of worse things than living out a life in these mountains. The Sierra Madres were beautiful.

We were coming close now, and we could see plenty of Apache sign. In gloomy places like this a body always had the feeling of being watched.

We drank, one at a time, with the others watching and in the saddle. We crossed the river then and went up a switchback trail for a thousand feet toward a tremendous promontory.

Storm clouds hung over the nearby peaks, and there was electricity in the air. Kahtenny's *rancheria* was somewhere below us, hidden in the low clouds. We started down through the trees, but had gone only a short distance when the rain began to fall in sheets, swept by a violent wind.

The forest offered slight cover, and there was nothing to do but hole up and wait it out. We found a place where a great pine had fallen almost to the ground, part of it resting among the rocks. We cut away the branches on the under side and took shelter there, lead-

ing our horses under cover with us. There was barely
room for us, and the pommel of my saddle brushed
the bark of the pine.

We took a chance, with the rain to keep down the
smoke and keep the Apaches under shelter, and built
a small fire where we made soup and coffee.

After a bit, with the rain still falling, I took up my
rifle and went out on a scout. Keeping to the trees, I
worked my way along the cliff. The rocks glistened with
wet, and the raindrops pelted my slicker like thrown
stones, but the trees offered some shelter.

Suddenly I was looking down into Kahtenny's
rancheria. There were a few smokes from wickiups, but
nobody was visible.

I felt a movement behind me, and I turned sharply.
It was Tampico Rocca.

He indicated the *rancheria* below us. "I could not
fool them now," he said. "They would smell the difference in me. I have been eating the white man's
food."

"How many would you guess there are?" I asked.
"Twenty, maybe?"

"Twenty, or twenty-five."

Two dozen human wolves . . . and I mean nothing
against them. My enemies for the time, yes . . . but
I respected them. At trailing or fighting they were fierce
and relentless as wolves; and we had done the impossible and followed them into their almost impregnable
Sierra Madre.

"I'm going down," I said. "I shall get close and
listen."

Rocca stared at me. "You crazy. They will hear you.
Their dogs will smell you."

"Maybe, but the rain will help."

"All right," he said, "we both go."

It would be a daring thing, but there was enough of
the Apache in him to be cautious. And it would be a
chance to count coups against the Apaches.

We crawled and slid down the mountain. From time
to time we paused to listen, then moved on. We were

fools, I told myself. What we did was insanity, no less. But I had to find Orry, and every hour in these mountains was an hour of danger for us . . . and for him.

Together we crept to the edge of the encampment in the driving rain. Rocca darted to the wall of one of the wickiups, and I went to another. Crouching in the rain, I listened, but heard nothing except the low mutter of Indian voices and the crackle of a fire. As I was moving to another, I was stopped for a moment by Rocca's uplifted finger. Hesitating, I watched him, holding my rifle, muzzle down under my slicker. He shook his head, and moved on. We had listened at five wickiups and were about ready to give up. . . . Suppose the children were not talking? Suppose they were not there at all?

Rocca gestured suddenly, and I went to him. We heard a mutter of talk within, and then, sure enough, a boy speaking plainly in English.

I caught Rocca's arm. "Cover me," I said, and lifting the flap, I stepped in.

For a moment I could see nothing, although I had taken the precaution of closing my eyes for a moment before stepping inside. Then in the red glow of the coals I saw a startled buck staring at me, and beginning to rise. On a pile of skins near one wall were three white children . . . I could just make them out.

A squaw was there, holding a child at her breast. She stared at me, no anger or hatred in her eyes, just a calm acceptance. "Do not cry out," I said in Apache. Then in the event she did not understand my poor use of the Apache tongue, I repeated it in Spanish.

The buck was past his astonishment, and he came at me with a lunge. I met him halfway with the butt of my rifle, and he went down in a heap, out cold.

"All right," I said to the children, "we're all going home. Wrap those skins around you and come on."

Turning to the young Indian woman, who had not stirred, I spoke quietly in Spanish. "I do not wish to hurt anybody. I want only to take these children home."

She merely looked at me as the three children ran

toward me. I saw that one of them was a girl. I waved
them past, toward the wickiup entrance, and they went
out quickly into the rain. With another glance at the
squaw, I followed.

Tampico Rocca was already hurrying the youngsters
toward the brush-clad hill where we had come down,
and he was backing away, covering the wickiups with
his rifle. I ran toward him, and was almost to the hillside when a man with a bloody head sprang from the
wickiup from which we had taken the children.

He leaped out, staggered, then glared wildly around.
His first yell failed him, but he shouted again and his
voice came full and strong. As he yelled he lifted his
rifle, and Rocca shot him.

The children were in the brush and climbing the
steep slope, faster than I would have believed possible.

Backing after them, I let the Apaches come boiling
out into the rain, and then fired rapidly.

One Indian spun and dropped his rifle; another yelled
and started for me. I let him come, and shot past him
at another who was lifting a rifle to fire. That Indian
staggered and fell, then started up again.

The running Indian had a knife, and he was almost
on me. Shortening my grip on my rifle, I took a long
swing that caught the running Indian in the belly. He
caved in with a choking cry, and I scrambled up the
muddy slope, grabbing at branches.

From above there was a sudden cannonade of fire
as our friends up there, who had heard the shooting,
opened up on the Indians to cover our retreat.

Scrambling, falling, and scrambling on, we made the
crest, and when the little girl fell I caught her up and
ran after Rocca, with the others covering us as best
they could.

We made our camp, swung into our saddles, and
with three of us each carrying a child, we raced off along
the ridge, rain whipping our faces.

We ran our horses when we could, then slowed for
the steep, dangerous trail down. Falling rain masked
the depths below; the great peaks were shrouded in

cloud. Thunder rumbled around us, tremendous sounds as if we were inside an enormous drum. We dashed into a pine forest, ran our horses for a hundred yards, then slowed for a steep slide and a muddy scramble.

Battles' horse slipped and fell, spilling him from the saddle, but the horse was game and scrambled up. By the time it was on its feet, Battles was in the saddle again.

There was no chance now for the black rock atop the boulder. Anyway, because of the rain Harry could not see it.

Me, I kept looking back over my shoulder, wondering when the Indians would catch up. The rain might have muffled the shots enough so that the other *rancherias* would not be alerted to our coming. We drew up briefly under the trees and I eased the girl into a better position on the saddle before me.

"Were there any other children back there?" I asked her. "White ones, I mean?"

"No," she said. Her eyes were bright, but she looked excited rather than scared.

"Which one is Orry Sackett?" I asked.

She just looked at me. "Neither one. Those two are the Creed boys. I never heard of any boy called Orry."

Something turned over inside me. "Tamp," I yelled, "my nephew isn't here!"

"I know it," he said. "He ain't here at all. These were the youngsters the 'Paches took. The only ones."

"That's not possible!"

"You better get goin'," Spanish said. "This here is no time to talk."

We started on, knowing there could be no hesitating, no turning back. The hills would be alive with Apaches now, and if we got out of here alive we'd have to have uncommon luck, which we had come into the mountains knowing.

Slipping and running, scrambling up and down muddy slopes, slapped by wet branches, racing through the forest . . . first and last, it was a nightmare.

We came finally to the place above the first Indian encampment, and I passed the girl over to Battles.

"I've got to get that boy Harry!" I told him.

"Don't be a fool! There's no chance!"

"Keep going," I said. "I promised him."

They all looked at me, each of them holding a youngster—three tough, hard-bitten men with no families, no homes, nothing to call their own but a set of guns and saddles. They sat there in the rain, and not one of them could come with me because now they had the children to think of.

"Run for it," I said. "This here's my scalp."

"Good luck," Spanish said, and they were gone.

Me, I watched them go, then swung my horse toward that boulder. Far back up the mountains, I thought I heard a shout and a shot. But I went down that trail to the place where I'd met the boy.

Rounding the boulder, rifle ready, I stared toward the *rancheria,* and suddenly out of the wet brush came the boy, Harry Brook. He was soaked to the skin and he was scared, but he came toward me. "Mister," he said, and he was crying. "Mister, I was scared you wouldn't make it."

Reaching down, I caught his hand and swung him up to the saddle.

"They know you're gone?" I asked.

"I think so . . . by now. Somebody came in and said he'd heard shootin', but the old bucks wouldn't believe him. No chance in this rain, they said, not in these mountains. I figured it was you, so first chance I had, I cut and run."

We started up the trail. Up there on the ridge I could see the muddy tracks of the other horses, and I swung into the trail after them, but then pulled up sharp. Their trail was almost wiped out by the track of other horses, unshod horses.

" 'Paches," I said. "Is there another trail?"

"Down there." The boy pointed toward the canyon. "The Old Ones' trail. An Apache boy showed it to me. It goes out across Sonora to the big water." Harry looked up at me, his face glistening with rain. "Anyway, that's what he said."

The black was fidgeting. He liked the situation no more than I did, so I pointed his nose where the boy said. He shied at the trail, then took it gingerly.

It was no kind of a place to ride even in good weather, let alone in a rain like this. Thunder crashed, and there was a vivid streak of lightning that lit up everything around. The trail was only a glistening thread along the face of a cliff.

But the black was game. He went as if stepping on eggs, but he went; and I held my breath for the three of us. Far down below my right stirrup I could see the tops of pine trees, maybe five hundred feet down there. We edged along, taking one careful step at a time, until we were almost at the bottom, when the trail widened out.

It took no time at all to see that this was no traveled trail. Rocks had fallen into it ages back, trees had grown up right in the middle, and we had to skirt around them. Me, I kept looking back. Sure as shootin' we were going to get ourselves trapped. Still, all a body could do was push on, so we pushed.

Night was a-coming, and with all those clouds and rain it was going to come soon, but there was no place to stop.

We had come down about a thousand feet, and were moving along a watercourse that wound through poplars and maples, gigantic agaves and clumps of maidenhair fern. Everything was wet.

Suddenly, off to our left, I saw one of those ruins—an ancient wall, half broken by a huge maple that had grown through it. There was a stream running that way, and it was only inches deep. Turning the black, I walked him along the stream until we could turn behind the wall where the maple grew.

There was a sort of clearing there, sheltered on one side by the wall, and falling away on the other toward a bigger stream; trees were all around. The maple had huge limbs that stretched out over the wall and made a shelter. I swung down under it and lifted the boy to the ground. "Stay up close to the tree," I said, "until I can rig something for us."

Now, a body doesn't spend his years wandering around the country without learning how to make do. I'd made wet camp a good many times before this, and I had been keeping my eyes open for a likely spot, one that had what we'd need.

First off, I saw how the ground slanted away toward the big creek, and I figured that wall offered fair protection. The maple was alive, but in some storm the wind had broken off a big limb, with a lot of branches on it, and it lay there on the ground. Maple burns mighty well, and makes a hot fire.

That big tree would give some shelter, and the wall would make a reflector for my fire. One branch of the tree extended across a corner of the wall, and I ducked under it and rolled away a couple of fallen stones that lay there. The big fallen limb and its branches offered partial cover for the corner, so I cut some pine branches and wove them in among the branches of the maple until I had a fair shelter.

Tying the black horse under the maple, but on a rope long enough so he could graze, I carried the saddle and gear to the shelter. The boy was already seated in the corner.

From under a couple of fallen trees I peeled some dry bark, gathered twigs from the fallen maple limb, and in a few minutes I had a fire going. It looked good, and felt better.

I had built the fire close against the wall so the heat would be reflected, and there we huddled in reasonable comfort. The wall, the sheltering trees, and our improvised shelter kept off most of the rain. After a few minutes, the boy fell asleep.

I checked my guns, made sure my rifle was fully loaded, and trusting to the black to warn me, I huddled against the wall on the opposite side of the fire from the boy, and slept too.

Chapter 8

THE NIGHT WIND moaned in the passes, and the small fire sputtered. The fuel burned down to coals, and the coals were a dull red except when touched briefly by the wind. The rain had come to an end, but big drops fell now and again from the leaves of the maple.

From time to time I opened my eyes, looked around, and slept again. It was always so with me . . . I can remember few nights when I slept the hours through without awakening, usually to lie awake listening for a while, sometimes to get up and prowl restlessly.

The black horse, now that the rain had stopped, moved away from the tree to crop the thick grass. Up on the ridges the grass had been sparse and had little nourishment, but the grass that grew around the fallen stones was rich and green.

You know how it is when you hear something a long time before you are really aware of it? It was like that now with riders coming down the trail. Most likely I didn't hear much . . . maybe only a whisper of sound . . . maybe some hidden sense felt the difference in the night; for they came like ghosts in the darkness, or like wolves, soft-footed and sure of their prey.

They must have been puzzled, and worried too, for I'd come down the trail of the Old Ones, where no one ever rode.

It was a spirit trail, and they would not have liked it, especially in the night. Their horses would be mountain-bred and sure-footed, and more than likely they had known this valley of the ruins when they ran wild, for there was grass here, good grass and water.

These riders must have been slow in getting away from their *rancheria,* coming after my tracks had crossed the trail of the Apaches that pursued my compadres. Seeing the tracks of my lone horse, they had followed, sure of a kill.

My small fire gave off so little smoke as to remain undetected, and its slight red glow would be hidden by the tree and the wall. Yet they found me. I suppose they heard my horse cropping grass.

All was still in my camp. A drop fell hissing into the coals, and my horse stopped cropping grass and lifted his head, blowing softly through his nostrils. I came clean awake.

An instant I lay there, listening, and then I rolled over and left the blanket in a long smooth dive into the darkness, and heard the whip of an arrow as I went. When I looked back, I saw that the arrow had gone through my blanket into the ground.

They came in fast, and my butt stroke missed the head of the nearest attacker, and hit his shoulder, staggering him. Then my rifle was knocked from my hands.

Now, back yonder in the mountains where I hail from, the boys and men do a sight of knuckle and skull thumping. The girls go to the dances for the dancing and the boys; and the boys go for the fighting and the girls.

Me being such a tall kind of homely boy, I had more time for fighting. Then in the Army, and on the river boats, and all—well, I'd done my share. So when I lost my rifle it just sort of freed me for fighting.

A body lunged against mine and I butted at the face, used my knee in his crotch, lifting him clean off the ground, so as I could lay hands on him. I fairly picked him up and threw him, and then I took a roundhouse swing at something coming at me. I saw a knife flash, and my fist landed and I felt bone crunch.

It was bang with both hands, swing, grab, butt. Apaches were fair hands at wrestling, but they had no experience at fist-fighting, and that was what I was doing. One short, powerful Apache grabbed me by the arm and the waist to throw me, but I brought my boot heel down on his instep and he let go and I could swing my elbow against his ear.

It was kind of lively there for a few minutes. There was three of them, but I was bigger and stronger. One of them jumped on my back with his forearm across my throat, but I grabbed his hand and elbow and flung him over my shoulder and smack down across the stone wall. He hit hard, and I heard him scream. And just then there was a shot.

Coming from outside of camp, it caught us unawares, but I saw an Apache fall and then the others ghosted into the night, one of them dragging the one I'd thrown across the wall. Then they disappeared like drops of water into a pool. They were there, and they were gone.

The one who had been shot was lying there near the fire, and Harry, his skins clutched around him, was sitting up, huddled and scared, in the corner of the wall.

And then a low voice said, "Hello, the camp!"

I said, "Come in, if you're of a mind to," and the next thing there walks into camp the cutest button of a girl you ever laid eyes on.

She was scarcely more than five feet tall and wore a buckskin hunting shirt that looked better than any such shirt I'd ever seen before. She was quick and pert, and she was leading her pony, but the Winchester in her hands wasn't for fun—that Apache would have realized it had he lived past her bullet.

She held out her hand. "I am Dorset Binny," she said, "and I hope you will forgive me for not looking as much like a lady as I should."

"Ma'am," I assured her, honestly enough, "when you come up like that and shoot that straight, I couldn't care how you're dressed."

And I added, "I am William Tell Sackett, and the boy yonder is Harry Brook, recently taken back from the Apaches."

We had both moved back into the shadows, and with that much said we took to listening. It was my idea those Apaches had them a bellyful, but they weren't alone, and this was no place to dally.

"Some other children got away, didn't they?"

"Yes—a couple of boys and a small girl."

"The girl was my sister. That is why I am here."

Well, she was talking to a shadow, for I was already saddling up. Right then, what I wanted between me and those Apaches was distance, for within a matter of hours this mountain would be alive with them, like a kicked anthill with ants.

She came along with me and the boy, and for an hour we followed the old trail north, then we turned west, taking a trail on which I found no tracks. Once in a while through the parted clouds I could see the sky, and sometimes a star was right above us. Black walls crowded closer, and we were skirting some almighty big boulders. Me, I kept thinking what a nasty place we were in, with the weather what it was. A body didn't need to look at the walls for a high-water mark. You just knew that the water must run through here thirty feet deep for an hour or two after a heavy storm. But the water had already passed on . . . and I wished for no more rain now.

The folks that had made this trail had no horses; it was a moccasin trail. After a while we had to get down and lead, for there was just no riding, but I let Harry stay on the black.

What I wanted most just now was to get out of these mountains and head off across the flatland, and maybe get to a ranch. But I had a time keeping my thoughts on my business with that girl along.

She was only a bit of a thing, but she must be packing a lot of nerve to come into this country after her sister. There was no chance to talk, for we were going single file, and I wasn't stopping. This was a strange trail, and we'd no idea where it might lead. Mayhap right into a bunch of Apaches—in which case some brave might have my scalp in his wickiup, if he bothered to take it. The Apaches were very strong on scalping.

At the top of a long slope we paused for a breather, and I looked around at Dorset. She was right behind me, leading her pony, and taking two steps to my one. Harry Brook, up there on the horse, had not said a word.

We stood there for a mite, and she said, "The sky's turning."

There was gray in it, all right, and day would come quickly now. We stood quiet then, saying nothing nor needing to, but there was communication in the night; we felt each other, felt the darkness and the danger around us, and felt the cool dampness of the canyon after the rain. We could smell the pines . . . and we smelled something else.

We smelled smoke.

It was enough to curl your hair. In this layout we couldn't expect friends. My partners had lit out to the north, I was sure, and if there was anybody here it had to be Apaches. And that smoke was right ahead of us.

We daren't go back, and we couldn't climb out. Me, I slipped the Winchester out of its scabbard, and so did she.

"We'll go ahead quiet," I whispered, "and if we can get by 'em, we will. Otherwise, we got to mount up and run for it. You and the boy get on the same horse, and if trouble shows, run."

"What about you?"

Me, I smiled. "Lady, you're not looking at no hero. I'll get off a few shots and I'll be dusting the trail right behind you, so don't slow up or I'll run right up your shirt tail."

We started on. Dawn was streaking the sky when we saw the canyon was starting to widen out. Then I saw moccasin tracks, some shreds of bark, and a few sticks—somebody collecting firewood. And then we heard yelling ahead of us, and I knew that kind of yelling.

"Might be," I said, "we can get by. They're mighty concerned, right now."

She looked at me. She said, "What concerns an Apache so much that we might slip by his camp?"

A man couldn't look into those honest gray eyes and lie. She would guess, anyway. "They got them a prisoner," I said, "and they're tryin' to find out how much of a man they caught. If he stands up to torture and dies well, they will figure they're big men, because they caught a big man."

We moved ahead, each of us warning our horse against noise; and those horses could be warned, they were that smart. Aside from their own instincts, they had caught some of our wariness for danger; for a horse, like a dog, can become extremely sensitive to the moods of his rider.

The western man trusted to his horse's ears, its eyes, its senses. He shared with it his water, and if need be, his food.

We moved forward quietly but steadily, and soon we saw their camp on a bench near the stream, partly hidden by brush and trees. The stream was not over four feet wide and no more than four or five inches deep, and the canyon through which we had come evidently caught the overflow.

Rifle ready, I led the way, watching the camp from the corner of my eye.

Here the dry stream-bed was perhaps fifty feet wide, most of it white sand dotted with rocks, many of them half buried. The brush was mostly willow, and thick.

It was a cool morning but I could feel sweat trickling down my back between my shoulder blades, and I worried for fear a hoof would strike stone. We went steadily on, drawing close to the camp, then abreast of it.

The Indians were almighty concerned with their prisoner, and they were shooting at him with arrows, missing him as close as they could, pinning the sides of his shirt to the tree, parting his hair with arrows. There was a trickle of blood down his forehead which I glimpsed when he lifted his head, and for the first time above their yells I heard his voice, and he was singing.

It was Spanish Murphy.

Yes, sir. Spanish was tied to a cottonwood in the clearing and the Apaches were shooting arrows at him and working themselves up to more serious ways of hurting . . . and he was singing!

Oh, they hated him for it, but they loved him for it, too, if I knew Indians. For their prisoner was a man with nerve, singing his defiance right into their faces . . . and it was also a means of keeping up his courage.

They would kill him, all right. They were devils when it came to inflicting pain, and they would try to make him last as long as possible, devising new tricks to give him the tortures of hell, and loving him for his strength and his guts.

Spanish was a singing man who loved the sound of the old songs, the western songs, the songs from the high-up hills. He was singing "Zebra Dun" when we caught sight of him and, raising his head, he looked right through an open space in the brush, looked right at us, and he changed his tune to "John Hardy."

"John Hardy was a desperate man, he carried his
   two guns every day.
He killed a man on the West Virginny line, but you ought
   to *see Tell Sackett gettin' away,*
I want to see Tell Sackett gettin' away!"

There he was, a-warning me. Him in all that trouble, but thinking most of us getting out of there. And me, I daren't stop, for I had a girl and a small boy depending on me. But this I did see. There weren't more than nine or ten Indians there, so far as I could see; they were all warriors.

We went on, our skins crawling with fear for Spanish Murphy, and also with fear for ourselves. We were beyond their camp now, but were expecting any moment to hear a yell behind us and to see the Apaches come streaming after us.

The thing that played into our hand was that the Indians probably had no idea there was anybody else about. They had either killed the others, or they'd taken out running.

Fifty yards beyond their camp the canyon took a bend, and when we had it behind us we felt some better.

I decided we didn't have much time before those 'Paches got down to serious business with Spanish. I knew I had to get him out of there, and I had to do it before he was hurt too bad to travel.

When we had gone a little way I pulled up. "You'll have to go on alone from here," I said to Dorset Binny. "Do you know Sonora?"

"No."

"The Apaches have run most of the folks off their ranches north of here, and the few who are still there won't fight back. I'd say ride due west and watch for a trail. If you can find a ranch, ask them to take you in and hide you."

She lingered, and I said, "Whatever made you try this, anyway?"

"There was nobody else to come. I didn't want my sister growing up an Apache." She hesitated. "Not that what we had was so much better. Since Pa died I've been trying to ranch, but we haven't done very well."

"You ride west," I repeated. "I don't need to tell you to be careful. You didn't get this far riding it blind."

I swung my horse, lifting a finger to my hatbrim. " 'Bye, Dorset."

"Good-bye, William Tell," she said, and they rode away up the canyon and I turned back.

I had no idea in my mind at all about what I was going to do. How does a body go about taking a prisoner away from blood-hungry Apaches? I couldn't just open fire. In the first place, they'd scatter out, pin me down, and surround me in no time. Also, they might just up and kill Spanish right off.

All the time there was a-nagging at me a thing I knew about Indians. Ninety-nine times out of a hundred a man who rides into an Indian camp is safe as long as he stays there—that is, if he rides in of his own notion, and not forced.

It was a long chance, for we were already shooting-enemies. They most likely knew me by sight by this time. Yet try as I might, I just couldn't come up with any other idea. But what to do when I got into their camp? How to get Spanish out of there?

I could get along in the language. Not that I was an easy talker like Tampico Rocca, but I could make out.

Spanish Murphy was in this fix because he had chosen to ride with me to Mexico, and it was up to me to take him from those Apaches, or to die with him.

I was packing plenty of iron. My Winchester was loaded, and I carried a six-shooter in my holster, with which I'd always been considered uncommonly swift. There was another six-shooter tucked into my belt.

So I swung my black horse up that bank and rode in amongst them.

For a minute there, you never saw anybody more surprised. These were Netdahee Apaches—killer warriors—dedicated to wiping out their enemies.

Now, as I've said, the Indian is a curious sort of man. They were bred to battle, and among the Apaches the Netdahee were the fiercest, a warrior society of chosen men. They appreciated nerve, but they were curious, and maybe they wanted to see what I was going to do. Maybe it was because I was inside their camp, but nobody lifted a hand.

My eyes took in the lot of them, methodically picking the ones at whom I would shoot first. If trouble started I'd have small time to pick targets, but if I could nail a few of them . . .

"Greetings!" I spoke to them in Apache. "I have come for my friend!"

Chapter 9

THEY TURNED LIKE tigers at bay, cornered, their black eyes staring. Of the nine of them, one was wearing an old Army coat, another a faded red shirt, and the others were naked except for breech-clouts and knee-high, Apache-style moccasins.

One held a rifle, two had pistols, and one held a bow and a handful of arrows. The others were armed only with their knives. Their rifles and bows lay near the fire.

The Apache with the bow and the one with the rifle, those I'd take first. An Apache can shoot his arrows just as fast as a man can work the lever on a Winchester . . . and they made a nastier wound.

"The man you have tied is my friend. We have come far together, and we have fought well together. He is a good man in the desert or in the mountains."

My sudden appearance had startled them, and they were unsure. Was I alone? I saw their eyes go to the rocks around their camp.

They could not believe I would ride into their camp alone. There was brush along both sides of the stream from where I had come, and the hills at this point were lower and covered with boulders.

They were all in front of me now, and I dared not ride among them. Taking my time, and lifting one hand to hold them as they were, I then lifted my rifle and pointed it at Spanish, then lowered the muzzle a trifle and fired.

My bullet cut the rope where it passed around the

tree to which Spanish was tied. He tugged, the rope loosened, and he tugged again.

Suddenly one of the Apaches moved. "Kill him!" he shrieked.

And I shot the man with the bow, then spurred the black and he leaped among them. I fired again, missed, and swung the stock of my rifle against an Apache skull. My horse went through them, turned swiftly, and started back.

A shot came from the rocks, then another. Spanish was loose and running toward the Apache horses.

A lean, fierce-looking Indian started for him and I held my sight an instant on his spine, then squeezed off the shot. The Apache kept running straight into a large boulder, hit it and seemed to rebound, then fell.

One Apache warrior made a running dive and sprang at me, grasping my saddle and swinging up to my horse, striving to get behind me.

I struck out savagely, guiding my horse with my knees, and for an instant we fought desperately. But I had both feet in my stirrups and a better purchase than he, so I threw him loose.

Spanish came charging from the horses, riding his own mount, and we went into the stream-bed side by side at a dead run, while the Apaches vanished into the rocks, shooting at the surrounding hills.

As we hit the sand of the stream-bed there was a rattle of rocks and, swinging around ready to fire, we saw Tampico Rocca and Battles riding neck and neck down the slope in a cascade of gravel.

We raced our horses for half a mile, then slowed to save them, and almost at once saw a fairly wide trail run off to the north from the stream. We took it, and crossed over a low hill into what must have been another part of the same stream-bed.

Then we held our horses to a good steady pace, keeping a sharp lookout behind. Nobody was talking. Me, I was watching the trail for some sign of Dorset and the boy, but we saw no tracks.

We were riding in the lower foothills of the Sierra

Madre now, and while the ridges were covered with pines, the lower slopes were a lush growth of maple, juniper, oak, and willow, with a thick underbrush of rose and hackberry. Small streams were frequent.

Somehow, more by chance than by skill, we had thrown them off our trail, but we knew better than to think it meant anything more than a breather. Surprise had worked for us, but the Apaches would find our trail, and they would catch up.

We lifted our horses into a trot, frequently glancing back over our shoulders, yet always watching the ridges around. We were now traversing a broken but relatively open country with trees along the streams or growing here and there in small clumps. After the heavy rains our passage raised no dust, and the hoofs of our horses made little sound in the grass.

Twice we forded streams, three times we rode upstream or downstream in the water to lose whatever trail we might leave.

Once in the shade of great arching trees, while giving our horses a breather and a chance to drink at a small stream, I told them about Dorset Binny and the boy. "If anything happens to me," I said, "find them and get them out of here."

The other youngsters had been riding quiet, scared and hungry, no doubt. Had it been us alone we'd never have chanced stopping to fix grub, but the children needed it, and we found ourselves a likely spot. While Rocca stood watch and Spanish fixed some food, Battles and me turned in under a tree for some sleep. It seemed like years since I'd caught more than a few catnaps.

When I woke up my mouth was dry, and I sat up, staring around, just taking stock. It was almighty quiet, a beautiful quiet such as you only find in the forest. Far off, we could hear the stir of wind in the pines, a wonderful sound. Closer to, there was only the murmur of water around the stones of the creek, and a faint chirping of birds. It was a natural, friendly quiet.

Tampico Rocca and Spanish came over to me. Battles was on lookout, perched up among the rocks where he could keep out of sight and still look the country over. The youngsters were sleeping.

"Got any idea where we are?" I asked Rocca.

"I been thinking on it." With his finger he drew a wavy line in the sand. "This here is the Bavispe," he said, and he pointed west. "She lies right yonder. If we cross the river there's some ranches. I wouldn't count on there being folks about, but it could be. Mostly the Apaches have wiped 'em out, burned 'em out, or stole them out. But it would be a good place to stop. There'll be old walls, water, and grass.

"Next we head for the Santa Margaritas . . . I know an old mining camp where we can hole up. Then we can head for Chinapa, on the Sonora River."

"Sounds good."

Spanish was chewing on a blade of grass. "Fact remains," he said, "that we didn't get what we come for. We didn't find your nephew."

Rocca was looking at me, watching me. "The little ones," he said, "they know nothing of such a boy . . . and they would know if the Indians had him."

"I put no faith in women," Spanish said, "meanin' no offense, but did you ever . . . I mean, you and your sister-in-law . . ."

I looked right at him. "I'll take no offense, Spanish— you've stood by me. I never saw her before we met in Tucson. I haven't seen my brother in some time . . . never did talk to him about his affairs. Little time we had together we mostly talked about the old days and what become of folks we knew." I looked around at them. "I ain't been home much. I've been drifting."

Nobody said anything for a while, and then Battles, who had come out of the brush, said, "I figure you've been lied to, Sackett."

"It don't make sense."

"Any reason she'd want you dead? You got to realize . . . not many come back from here. We ain't even sure we're gettin' back."

"The children never heard of any other boy," Rocca repeated, "and they'd know. And, Harry Brook would.

He speaks the language pretty good, and there's talk around the Indian villages."

Well, there was no use studying on it now. We had miles to travel. I said as much and we saddled up and moved down the creek.

Rocca rode with his head over his shoulder. I mean he was a worried man. When you see Apaches you're worried, but when you don't see them you're maybe really in trouble. They could be all around you.

When the shadows were beginning to reach out from the hills we came up to a ranch, four tired men with some tired children. As we neared it we spread out and I rode with my Winchester up in my hands, my eyes moving under the low brim of my hat, searching each shadow, each doubtful place.

No smoke . . . no movement. Somewhere a blue jay fussed, somewhere a quail called into the stillness and another made reply. Otherwise it was still.

Nobody spoke, and we rode into the yard. Battles rode through the gate, and I went through a gap in the ruined wall. Spanish circled to the right. Rocca to the left.

The ranch was deserted . . . a ruin. Fire had gutted it, and some of the stone walls had toppled. The windows gapped like great, hollow eyes that stared upon nothing. The barns were a tumbled mass of burned timbers and the fallen stones of foundation walls. Mesquite trees choked up the corrals.

But trees still shaded the ranch yard. Water ran from an iron pipe into a tank. An oak limb had grown through an open window. In the patio the blocks of stone that paved it had been thrust up by a growing sycamore, which was now several inches through.

Once this ranch had been a splendid place, once the fields had been green and men had worked here, lived here, and loved here.

We rode into the thick grass where the ranch yard had been and we drew up. We heard only the wind . . . only the trickle of water into the tank.

John J. Battles looked slowly around and said nothing, and Spanish Murphy sat silent for a long moment. Then he said, "This is the sort of place you dream about, when you're on a long, dusty trail, or you're in the desert and short of water."

"We'd better have a look around," I said. "Tamp, you scout to the wall yonder. Spanish can stay with the children."

We moved out. A rabbit sprang from under my feet and went bounding away. We searched the place, but we found nothing, nothing at all.

There was a watch tower on one corner of the place, shrewdly built to observe the country around, but now partly masked by the tops of trees. While I took the first watch, Battles put some grub together for a meal.

The sun was warm and pleasant, but it bothered me for I could see too little in the open country to the west. Our enemies should come from the east, but trust an Apache to use the sun's glare if he figured on an attack. But the sun sank behind the mountains to to westward and I studied the country all around with great care, and saw nothing.

Where were Dorset Binny and the boy? If they had ridden the way we planned they should be not too far away, for our course had veered around and we, too, had come west.

From the watch tower I could study the terrain and my eyes searched out all possible hiding places. The position of the ranch had been well chosen. The place had a good field of fire in every direction and must have been easy to defend back in the old days, yet the Indians had taken it, burned it out, and more than likely killed everybody on the ranch.

It seemed to me at least fifteen to twenty men would have been needed to defend the ranch. Maybe they were shorthanded when the attack came.

In the last minutes of daylight, I saw them coming—two riders, not over half a mile off.

I called softly to Murphy, who was closest and knelt by one of the openings left in the wall for a firing position. But I was sure right from the start. As they drew nearer I could see them clear enough.

Standing up on the tower I called out, "Dorset! Dorset Binny! Come on in!"

Chapter 10

LAURA PRITTS SACKETT was immaculate. She was cool, aloof, yet she managed to convey the idea that beneath that still surface there was turmoil, waiting to be exploited. A cold, emotionless young woman, she had learned very early that the appearance of deep emotion and passion beneath the quiet exterior was a tool and a weapon to be used, and so she had used it.

Her adoration for her father had resulted in hatred for all who in any way thwarted or opposed him.

As the days passed into weeks and she heard nothing from Mexico, she grew worried. Suppose, after all, Tell Sackett was not killed by the Apaches? Suppose he did return, and her falsehood was exposed? She was less worried, however, about being exposed—she had no intention of remaining in Tucson anyway—than about Sackett not being killed.

She knew enough about the Sacketts to know they had a way of getting out of corners. Suddenly, she made up her mind.

She would leave Tucson. She would go back east without waiting any longer. She might never hear what happened in Sonora, and there was no sense in staying on here, in this heat, and merely waiting. Her father had a little property in the East, and it was time she returned to settle the estate. But first she would make one final effort.

She was seated in the Shoo-Fly when she reached that decision. She knew, as did everyone, about the

81

gun battle in the Quartz Rock Saloon, and she had seen the Hadden boys around town. She knew also that the Haddens had been doing some talking about what would happen when they met Tell Sackett and Tampico Rocca again.

Suddenly the door opened and Captain Lewiston came in, accompanied by Lieutenant Jack Davis, whom she remembered from the stage ride to Tucson.

They came to her table. "Mrs. Sackett," Davis said, "I want to present Captain Lewiston."

She turned her wide blue eyes on the Captain and sensed a coolness, a reserve. This one would not be so easy as Davis to wind around her finger. "How do you do, Captain," she said. "Won't you sit down?"

The men seated themselves and ordered coffee. "I hope you will forgive the intrusion, Mrs. Sackett," Captain Lewiston said, "but we were wondering if you could tell us anything about the present location of Tell Sackett. I believe he is a relative of yours."

"He is my brother-in-law," she said, "although I had never met him until a few weeks ago. Right here in this room, in fact. He was with some other men. I don't know where they went. Is he in trouble?"

Lewiston hesitated. "Yes and no," he said finally. "If he rode into Apache country, as we have heard that he did, he may be in very serious trouble indeed."

She allowed her lip to tremble. "He . . . he hasn't been killed, has he? The Sacketts are reckless, daring men, and . . ." She let her words trail away.

"We have heard nothing," Lewiston said. "We are planning a strike against the Apaches that will take us deep into Mexico. We would not want them stirred up by some unauthorized foray into their country."

"I . . . I did not know. If anything should happen to Mr. Sackett my husband would be very upset. They are very close."

"Mrs. Sackett, I understand you provided Mr. Sackett with a horse? Is that true?"

"Of course. His own had been killed and he was unable to purchase one. I merely helped." She smiled. "What else could I do?"

Lewiston was not satisfied, yet there was certainly nothing wrong with her story, nor had he any reason to suspect she knew Tell Sackett's whereabouts, except the fact that they were relatives, and had talked together. He could not have given any reason for his dissatisfaction, but he felt it. Moreover, he had liked Tell, and he was worried about him.

Later he said as much to Davis. "Oh, come now, Captain!" Davis said. "If Laura Sackett knew anything about Sackett she would tell you. What possible reason would she have for lying?"

"I don't know. But why is she staying on in Tucson? She has no relatives here, no friends, and this is no time of year to be here if you can be anywhere else. I mean, I like the place, but not many eastern women such as Laura Sackett are inclined to want to stay here."

Davis had done some wondering about that himself. Tucson was a hot, dusty little desert town, and not a likely place for a lady of aristocratic background such as Laura had implied in a few carefully casual references. A stopover to recover from the rigors of a stage trip from California would be natural, but the days had stretched on, and still she remained. Had she been known in the area or had friends there, her presence would have been no cause for comment, but she kept very much to herself and indicated no desire to make acquaintances.

Laura was unconcerned as to what anyone thought. She detested Tucson and its people, and wanted nothing so much as to go on to El Paso and thence to New Orleans and the East. If she could only be sure Tell Sackett was dead she would leave.

She knew what she must do. Tell Sackett had now been gone for three weeks, and while it seemed likely that he was dead, he might even now be coming north over the trails through Sonora. So she had one more thing to do. She had to make sure that, if he had lived through the journey into the Apache stronghold, he would die before getting back to Tucson. Somehow she must manage to talk with Arch or Wolf Hadden.

They came rarely to the Shoo-Fly. There were other places to eat among their own kind, and she had seen them on the streets with other toughs of ugly reputation. By listening to talk she heard around her, she learned that the Haddens were, among other things, bronc riders and wild-horse hunters. They had come into town with several horses for sale or trade.

She spoke to Mrs. Wallen quite casually. "There is a man about town," she said, "a rough-looking man named Hadden, who has a sorrel gelding for sale. I would like to talk to him."

Mrs. Wallen hesitated, putting her hands on her hips. "Ma'am, those Haddens are not fit men for a lady to know. I will have Mr. Wallen talk to them."

"If you please," Laura Sackett answered coolly, "I would prefer to talk to them myself. I have dealt with many rough men whom my father employed. I have also had some experience in buying horses."

"Very well," Mrs. Wallen replied stiffly, "have it your own way."

Laura was amused. Mrs. Wallen did not like her, she knew, and Laura cared not at all, but it made her feel good to put her in her place, if ever so gently.

She finished her tea and, getting to her feet, she gathered her skirt in one dainty gloved hand and went out on the boardwalk. The heat struck her face like heat from the open door of a furnace. She stood an instant, looking up and down the street, and then she went on to her rooming house.

Arch Hadden was seated on the steps. He got to his feet as she approached. "Wallen said you wanted to see me about a horse."

She studied him for a moment. "About a horse," she said, "and some other matters. If you will saddle that sorrel you have and bring him around in the morning I shall ride out with you. If the horse is satisfactory, I will buy him."

The next morning in the early coolness they rode

out beyond the mission. The little sorrel moved well, but Laura was not interested in the horse. In a thick grove of cactus and brush, she drew up and Arch Hadden rode up close beside her.

He looked at her with a knowing leer. "Ma'am, I reckon you come to the right man. Now I'll just get down an' he'p you off that horse. . . ."

In her hand she held a two-barreled derringer. "Stay right where you are, Hadden," she said. "I brought you out here to talk to you. Do you know what my name is?"

He stared at her, puzzled but wary. "Can't say as I do. At the livery stable Wallen just told me to come and see the blonde lady at that roomin' house. I reckon ever'body in town has seen you, ma'am."

"I am Laura Pritts Sackett."

His face sharpened suddenly as if the skin had drawn tight. He was very still, and with amusement she could see what was happening in his mind. She was a woman, and she had a gun on him. She could kill him and say he had attacked her, and she would not be blamed; but if he drew on her and killed her, he would be hung for murder.

"Don't be frightened, Hadden. I am not going to kill you. In fact, I want you to kill somebody for me—for both of us."

"What's that mean?"

"There is a man who has gone down into Mexico and I think the Apaches may have killed him, but if he should be coming back I want him killed before he reaches Tucson."

Hadden shook his head. "I've killed a few men," he said, "but only in fights. I ain't no paid killer, ma'am."

"Not even if the man is Tell Sackett?"

He was still wary, but interested. "You askin' me that? And you a Sackett?"

"I am not a Sackett, Hadden. I had the misfortune to marry one. I married him to help my father, but they turned on him anyway. Tell Sackett is my brother-in-law, and I want him killed, Hadden.

"There are men in this town, Hadden, who would kill a man for fifty dollars, and there are others all along the border. I will give you two hundred dollars if you will bring me evidence that Tell Sackett is dead. I don't care whether you kill him or somebody else does. All I want is proof."

Hadden rested his palms on the saddle horn and chewed on his mustache. He had heard that Sackett had ridden south, but he also knew that Spanish Murphy, who had ridden with him, had told some friends in Mex town that he would be back in a few weeks.

Arch Hadden was a hard, tough man, and a bitter one. He had ridden into Tucson hunting John J. Battles, an old enemy. He had decided to kill Tampico Rocca, knowing nothing about him, because Rocca was Battles' friend and it would bring Battles out of hiding. Tell Sackett had simply been a stranger of whom he had known nothing. Since the gun battle in which Arch Hadden had been so roughly treated and one of his men had been killed, another seriously wounded, he had heard a lot about the Sacketts. He wanted to kill Tell Sackett, but he was no longer at all sure he could kill him in a stand-up gun fight. On the other hand, here was an offer of two hundred dollars, representing six months' hard work on the cattle ranges, for killing him, money it would be a pleasure to earn.

Slowly, he dug out the makings and rolled a smoke. Laura Sackett seemed in no hurry, and Arch wanted to think this thing through.

"There would be no trouble for you, Hadden," she persisted. "You have already had a fight with him. If there is another fight and you kill him, nobody would be surprised."

"Why'd you pick on me?"

"You're the obvious one. He bested you. You want him beaten or dead. You are the one who can do it and no questions asked."

"How you figure to pay me?"

"I will give you one hundred dollars now, and the

other hundred will be left at the Wells-Fargo office to be delivered to you by my order."

"Won't folks wonder why you're payin' me money?"

"No. You will be rounding up and breaking four horses for me, to be delivered in El Paso. The money would be in payment for that."

Grimly, he stared at her. The derringer was still in her hand, and now he knew she would shoot if need be. Not that there would be any cause for it, but this was a dangerous woman.

"Supposin' I was to take your hundred dollars an' ride off?" he suggested.

She smiled. "Hadden, my father and I were in the land grant wars in New Mexico. We had occasion to hire men who could use their guns. I have told you there are plenty of men along the border who would kill for fifty dollars. If you took my money without trying to make good on it, I would hire four separate killers and send them out with good rifles to get you— and they would, Hadden."

He chuckled. "I just wondered. All right, ma'am, I'll take the hundred. I been figurin' on killin' Sackett, an' this here will pay expenses while I do it."

She rode back to town with Hadden trailing behind, and at the livery stable, before witnesses, she said, "I do not like the sorrel, Hadden, but I do want four horses delivered to me in El Paso. I will pay you one hundred dollars now, the other hundred to be paid by Wells Fargo on my authorization when the horses are delivered."

Arch Hadden stabled his horses and went outside. He rolled another smoke, lit the cigarette, and drew deeply. This was money he was going to enjoy earning. He looked around and saw Wolf approaching. "Wolf, we got us a job," he said. "We got us a good job."

Chapter 11

WE PASSED a quiet night. Until the last of the twilight was gone I could still hear the quail. These were the Mexican blue quail that run along the ground more than they fly, ofttimes thirty or forty of them in a covey.

Around a small fire, we talked it over. We had invaded Apache country and taken prisoners from them, so they would be on our trail, they would never let up.

The horses needed rest. The deserted ranch had water and plenty of good grass, and there was a good field of fire. We decided to stay put, and that was all right with me. I'd seen no such beautiful place in all my life, and I said as much to Dorset.

"It *is* beautiful," she agreed, "and peaceful. I wonder they ever left . . . the people who lived here."

"Apaches. They devastated this whole stretch of country. Folks tried again and again to build homes here, but they couldn't make it.

"When we leave here," I went on, "we're going to have to run. It is going to be pure hell betwixt here and the border towns."

"Why did she do it, Tell?" Dorset asked suddenly. "Why did she want you killed?"

"I don't know that she did."

"There was no Orry Sackett, Tell. Can't you see that? She lied to you. All the children are accounted for. There were the Creed youngsters and my sister. Harry had been taken long before, and there simply were no others."

88

This idea about Orry worried me. It was something that needed contemplating, but there was another worry in what Dorset said; for if there was no child, why send me skyhootin' into such dangerous country? Unless she did want me dead? And if she wanted me dead, would she stop with this? Suppose she tried again to kill me when I showed up alive . . . if I did?

I never was much good at thinking complicated things out. Mostly I studied on situations and then went ahead and did what I would have done, anyway. When it comes to work and travel or a fighting situation, I can come up with answers, but I never was any good at figuring out why folks turned to evil.

"Dorset," I said, "I can't think of a reason why anybody should want me killed like that. Why, she might be the death of these men with me, too."

"Maybe she wants to get back at your brother. Maybe she hates the name of Sackett."

It made no kind of sense, but I had one thought a body couldn't get around. And that was that she had sent me off to Mexico after a child who I now felt sure never existed.

You might figure I could have looked around more, but not if you knew Apaches. If any Apaches had a white prisoner it would be known to all of them. They had few secrets among themselves. So I was left with the almost certain knowledge that I'd been sent down here on a wild-goose chase that would be almost sure to get me killed.

Nor was there much I could do about it if I got back. She would simply say that I lied, that she had told me no such thing—if she was even around to be accused.

And she would know I wasn't going to beat up a woman or shoot her. We Sacketts treated womenfolk gentle, even when they didn't deserve it.

Had it been only me, I'd have figured I'd been played for a sucker and I'd have let it go at that, though it wouldn't have been a pretty thought. But she had risked the lives of my friends.

We laid up at that deserted ranch for three days. It wasn't only that we needed the rest, or that our horses did. It was because a man who doesn't travel doesn't leave any trail. And those Apaches would be looking for a trail. They would figure that we would naturally high-tail it for the border, and when the trail was lost they'd head for the border by several trails, exchanging smokes to talk across the country. So by laying low at this ranch we left them with no trail to see, and the feeling that we had taken some other, unknown route.

On the morning of the fourth day we moved out. Tampico Rocca knew of a ranch twenty-odd miles west, and we headed for that, keeping off the ridges and using every trick we knew to cover our sign.

But we weren't trusting to that. We rode with our eyes looking all around all the time, and our rifles across our saddles. We rode loose and we made pretty good time all the first day, wanting distance behind us.

It was rough country. You've got to see some of that country to believe it. Water was growing scarcer, there were fewer trees except along the river bottoms, and there was more cactus. We saw antelope now and again, and once, passing through a rugged stretch of bare rock mountains, we saw some desert bighorns. They're pretty near the finest meat the country offered, but we weren't about to shoot a rifle.

When we reached the ranch we found that it was a big one, and it lay right out in the open country, with a small stream winding past. There was a dam across the stream and a fair-sized pond had backed up behind it. Cottonwoods and other trees grew around, and a big Spanish-style ranch house was set amongst them. And it was occupied.

We drew up on the crest of a low ridge among some ocotillo and other growth and studied the layout. We weren't going to ride up to any place without giving thought to what lay before us.

Slow smoke was rising from the chimney, and we could hear the squeak of a windlass as somebody pulled water at a well. We could see a couple of vaqueros riding out of the back gate, heading for the hills to the southeast of us. They were riding relaxed and easy, sitting lazy in the saddle as if neither of them had ever known a care or the name of trouble.

We came down off the slope, riding scattered out a little until we were channeled by a lane through wide fields of planting.

"Somebody watches us." Rocca indicated a low tower, and we could see sunlight gleam on a fieldglass or telescope.

Whoever it was must have seen the children and decided we could be trusted, because the big wooden gates opened, although nobody was in sight. But as we drew closer we could see the black muzzles of the rifles that covered our approach.

We rode in through the gates and they closed behind us. At least six vaqueros were now in sight, and standing on the wide veranda, a thin Cuban cigar in his teeth, was a tall old man with white hair and an erect, proud figure.

He came down two steps to greet us, his sharp eyes taking us in with quick intelligence. I think he knew our story before I spoke, for the hard-ridden horses, and the children, one of them dressed like an Apache boy, told it.

"*Buenos dias, señores,*" he said, and then added in English, "My house is yours."

"You may not wish us to stay, *señor,*" I said. "We have taken these children from the Apaches, and they will be looking for us."

"They have visited us before, and with less reason. You are my guests, gentlemen. I am Don Louis Cisneros."

"I am Tell Sackett," I said, and introduced the others.

He greeted them and then turned his eyes to me. "Yours is a familiar name," he said. "There was a Sackett who married the granddaughter of an old friend."

"That would be my younger brother, Tyrel. He married into the Alvarado family."

"Come in," he said, and as we walked into the dim coolness of the interior, he added, "We are old friends, my family and the Alvarados. I have heard much of your family, *amigo*. Your brother stood between Alvarado and his enemies."

Hours later, when we had bathed and eaten a good dinner at his table, we sat about smoking the Don's Cuban cigars. I was never much of a hand to smoke, but did from time to time, and this was one time I joined in.

Dorset and the children had gone off with the Don's daughters, and the boys and me we stayed with our host.

"You have a dangerous road before you. I can let you have a dozen riders," he said.

"No. You may need them. We've come this far, and we'll ride on." Sitting back in the big cowhide chair, I told him the whole story, and he listened without comment. At the end he said nothing for several minutes.

"I have news of your family. I wish you could have known it sooner. The woman you speak of was married to your brother Orrin, but they have separated. She was the daughter of Jonathan Pritts, the man who led the men who tried to seize the Alvarado Grant. It was your brother Tyrel who led the fight that defeated him, and when Orrin found his wife was involved, he left her. She has hatred for all who bear the name of Sackett. You were to be killed, *amigo*."

It seemed unreasonable that a woman would go to such lengths to get a man killed, a man who had done her no harm, but it all tied up into a neat package. And there wasn't much I could do about it. Maybe the best way to get even would be just to get back alive, so all her plotting would come to nothing.

In the quiet of the lovely old hacienda, all that lay outside seemed far away, not something that lurked just beyond the adobe walls. But deep in our hearts not one of us thought himself free of what was to come.

The miles of the desert that lay between us and the relative safety of Tucson could be nightmare miles. They were ever-present in our minds, but they were a fact of our lives to be taken in stride.

Old Don Luis talked quietly and easily of the problems of living among the Apaches. As Pete Kitchen had survived north of the border, so had he survived south of it. He had his own small army of tough, seasoned vaqueros, fighters every one of them.

As he talked he glanced over at Rocca. "If you ever want a job, *señor*," he said, "come to me here. There is a place for you. I have two vaqueros here who grew up with the Apaches."

"It is a good place," Rocca said. "It may be that one day I shall come riding here."

Long after the others had turned in, I sat in the quiet of the old Don's study and talked with him. The walls of the room were lined with shelves of leather-bound books, more than I had ever seen, and he talked of them and of what they had told him, and of what they meant to him.

"These are my world," he said. "Had I been born in another time or to another way of life I should have been a scholar. My father had this place and he needed sons to carry on, so I came back from Spain to this place. It has been good to me. I have seen my crops grow and my herds increase, and if I have not written words upon paper as I should like to have done, I have written large upon the page of life that was left open for me.

"There is tonic in this." He gestured toward the out-of-doors. "I have used the plow and the Winchester instead of the pen and the inkstand. There is tonic in the riding, in the living dangerously, in the building of something.

"I know how the Apache feels. He loves his land as I do, and now he sees another way of life supplanting his. The wise ones know they can neither win nor last, but it is not we who destroy them, but the times.

"All things change. One species gives way to another

better equipped to survive. Their world is going, but
they brought destruction to another when they came,
and just so will we one day be forced out by others
who will come. It is the way of the world; the one thing
we know is that all things change.

"Each of us in his own way wars against change.
Even those who fancy themselves the most progressive
will fight against other kinds of progress, for each of
us is convinced that our way is the best way.

"I have lived well here. I should like to see this last
because I have built it strong and made it good, but I
know it will not. Even my books may not last, but the
ideas will endure. It is easy to destroy a book, but an
idea once implanted has roots no man can utterly destroy."

He paused and looked at me. "You are bored with
an old man talking."

"No, sir. I am learning. We are a people who have
hungered after learning, Don Luis, and who have had
too little of it. I mean we Sacketts. Our mountain lands
had thin soil, and they gave us nothing more than just
a living until we came west."

I looked at him and felt ashamed. "I can barely
read, sir. It is a struggle to make out the words, and
what they mean. Some I hunt down like a coyote after
a rabbit. I look at those books with longing, sir, and
think of all the things they might say to me."

I got up, for of a sudden there was a heavy weariness
upon me. "My books have been the mountains," I said.
"The desert, the forest, and the wide places where the
grass grows. I must learn what I can from the reading
I can do."

Don Luis got up also, holding out his hand. "Each of
us must find wisdom in his own way. Mine is one way,
yours another. Perhaps we each need more of what the
other knows. . . . Good night, *señor*."

When I went outside I walked through the gate to
smell the wind, to test the night. By the wall near me
a cigarette glowed, cupped in a hand.

"How goes the watch?" I asked in Spanish.

"Well, *señor*." He held the cigarette behind the wall in the darkness. He bowed his head and drew deep; the small red fire glowed and faded again. "We are not alone, *señor*. Your friends and ours, they are out there . . . waiting."

So they had caught up with us. Now there would be hell to pay in Sonora.

Turning on my heel, I went back into the house. The old Don was just leaving his study.

"You have many horses?" I asked.

"All you need," he assured me.

"Can you give us three apiece? I can't pay you now, but—"

"Do not speak of pay," he interrupted. "Your brother is the husband of my old friend's granddaughter. You may have the horses." He looked closely at me. "What will you do?"

"Your vaquero says they are waiting out there now. I think he is right. And so I think we will take our chances and run for it. We'll switch horses without stopping . . . maybe we can outdistance them."

Don Luis Cisneros shrugged. "You might," he said. "I will have the horses ready at daybreak."

"An hour before," I said. "And *gracias*."

Chapter 12

THE HORSES were ready and we were mounted, the children with us. The Don's men were posted on the walls to cover our going. My horse was restive, eager to be away, but I glanced around at Dorset. In the vague light her face seemed pale, her eyes unusually large. I suspected mine were the same.

"The tall pine yonder," I said, and pointed in the direction. "Ride for it, ride hard. They will be close around, with their horses well back from where they wait. With luck, we can ride through them and be away before they can get off more than a shot or two."

Sixteen men were on the walls, rifles ready for firing. Other men stood by the gates, prepared to swing them open.

Don Luis walked over to me and held up his hand, and I took it. *"Vaya con dios, amigo,"* he said gravely, and then he lifted a hand to the men at the gates and they swung them wide.

We went through the gates with a rush at the same instant as all sixteen men fired. Some had targets chosen, having spotted lurking Apaches, others fired at bits of likely cover.

We hit the trail running, with Spanish Murphy and myself in the lead. I saw the dark form of an Apache rise up almost directly before me and chopped down to fire with my pistol, but the horse struck him and knocked him rolling. A hoof spurned his body, and then we were past and running, with the vaqueros on the wall picking targets from those we drove from hiding.

The tall pine was a mile off, and we rode directly for it through the half-light of the early dawn. We covered that mile at a dead run, slowing to a trot as we neared the tree. I glanced around swiftly.

"How is it? Are we all here?" I asked.

"I was the last one," Battles said. "We all made it."

"Anybody hurt?"

"They burned my shoulder," Rocca said. "It is nothing."

So I led them away at a fast trot for a little way, then I ran the horses again for a good half-mile, slowed to a trot and then a walk, then ran them again.

At noon we drew up at a small seep that came from the base of a grass-covered dune. We watered our horses, exchanged saddles to fresh horses, and pushed on.

We kept a good pace, riding wide of any places of ambush, and watching for dust clouds. There were bandits as well as Indians to be feared, and there were soldiers, too, who might resent our being here. All this while the children did not cry, they did not once call out. The Apaches had taught them that, if nothing more.

At midafternoon we rode into a deserted village. The ruins of a large adobe still stood, and a half-completed church. There was water running in an irrigation ditch.

In a corner of one of the houses was a skeleton, still half-clothed, of a Mexican who had died fighting. The left arm of the skeleton showed a break that had mended badly, leaving the arm shorter and crooked.

Tampico looked at it then at the dried leather of the holster on which an initial had been carved. It was a large B.

"So this is where it happened, Benito," he said, and then glancing around at me, he said, "I knew him. He was a bad one, but brave."

We made coffee there, and a hot soup from the jerked beef, and some corn, potatoes, and onions found in the deserted fields, now gone to weeds. We ate quickly, but we ate well.

Spanish wiped his hands on his chaps and looked at me. "Let's be gettin' on," he said. "There's a smell of death about this place."

John J. Battles was already in his saddle, waiting. We mounted up and moved out, riding fresh horses again, so as to use none of them too hard.

It was hot and still in those late hours of the day, and the dust did not rise. Suddenly Murphy indicated a place on the horizon where a blue-gray finger of smoke made a question mark against the mountains. It was ahead of us off to the east. We knew what it meant, and we pressed on, picking up the north star for guiding, following it as best we could, with what the terrain offered.

After midnight we stopped among some willows and made dry camp in an arroyo.

Short of daybreak we were in the saddle again, and pushing on. We passed a village off to our right.

"Tres Alamos," Rocca said. Three Cottonwoods . . . it was the name of many villages. Later we passed near another village, but avoided it, for there was no time for answering questions, and they would not like us bringing the Apaches on them. This was Senokipe—hollow tree.

I loved the names the country gave, the sound of them made music to the ear. Santa Rosalia . . . Soledad . . . Remedios . . . Soyopa . . . Nacori . . . Chimala . . . Kiburi. Okitoa, a sparrow hawk's nest; Batuco, a waterhole; Cumuripa, a rathole . . . Matape, the red cliff; and Bacadeguatzi, meaning "at the white mountain." The men who came first to this land used the names descriptive of it, the names that grew as naturally from the land as the cottonwood, the willow, or the ocotillo.

Dawn came up in crimson light over the eastern mountains; it flushed the mountainsides with a kind of dull flame.

"I don't like it," Rocca muttered gloomily. "It looks like blood."

In the next hour we counted three smokes . . . three and an answering smoke.

We stopped at a small creek, watered the horses, and shifted saddles.

"If anything goes wrong," I said to Dorset, "you take the children and ride for the border. Harry can handle his own horse and one of the youngsters."

Rocca turned in his saddle. "I can smell Apaches. They have been by this way, and not long since."

Murphy chuckled. "You're dreamin', boy. Nobody can smell that good."

"They have been here," Rocca insisted. "And they will come again."

Now that we were further north, the grass was sparser, there were bare sandhills, and the bare brown-red rock of the mountains was streaked with the white of quartz. The sun was hot two hours before noon. The air was still; nothing stirred anywhere. Dancing heat waves emphasized the dead quiet.

My skin crawled. Again and again I shifted my rifle to wipe the sweat from my hands. Sweat streaked the dust on the faces of my companions, and the sweat trickling down my spine was cold and clammy under the slight stir of wind. I tried to assay our chances and came up empty.

John J. Battles suddenly spoke. "I'd like to see the leaves turning red and gold again, and hear the wild geese honk."

"You're thinking of a northern land," Spanish Murphy said. "I remember a time like that in Wyomin'. I drove a herd east from Oregon."

Dorset edged close to me. "Tell," she said softly, "do you think we'll make it?"

I did not want to talk; it was a time for listening. "We've had luck so far," I answered.

We switched horses again and pushed on through the nooning time—four bold but lonely men, a girl scarcely become a woman, and the youngsters, four of them. With the spare horses, three per rider, and our pack horse, we made a solid bunch. Our other pack horse had long since been lost.

Somewhere, still far off to north of us, lay the border,

a thin line drawn on maps, and a thin line in our consciousness, but a strong one across our lives. North of it there might be help. And further north still there was sanctuary.

We slowed the horses to a walk. It was very hot. The sun was lost in a brassy sky.

I think we all knew that the Apaches would come. We could elude a few, but we could not elude them all. The Apache had no regard for horse flesh. He would ride a horse to death and then eat him, so he rode often at a killing pace. And there were the talking smokes, speaking across the distance.

I did not hate the Apache. He was my enemy as I was his because of the time and the circumstances; but he was a fighting man, and a strong man who endured much to live in this country. If they captured us they would kill us. There would be torture for the men, worse perhaps for the girl, but it was their way of life, and you judge each man by his time and his way of life.

We walked our horses while the saddles creaked, and we blinked our eyes to see past the sting of the salty sweat trickling into them. Dark stains showed on our shirts. We drank water from our canteens, and kept on.

We knew there was a waterhole ahead. Rocca knew where it lay, Spanish knew, and I knew. We thinned out as we rode nearer, and we cut for sign, but found none. We could see a cottonwood up ahead, and a small clump of willows. Off to the east, fifty yards or more from the waterhole, rose a bare upthrust of rocks perhaps half a mile long, and not more than a hundred yards wide for most of its length.

Pulling up, I studied those rocks. "That waterhole now," I said. "If somebody was up in those rocks anybody at the waterhole would be a sitting duck."

"We got to have water," Murphy said.

Glancing around, I saw a separate small island of rocks rising perhaps from a buried spur of the ridge. "You folks hole up over yonder," I said, "and I'll take three horses and the canteens and ride over there for water. You cover me. If any shooting starts, you open up on the ridge over there. I'll water the horses, and fill the canteens."

Leading the horses, I rode to the waterhole. There was a desert wren singing in the willows, and the cottonwood leaves were rustling, as they do in the slightest breeze. Some quail sifted away through the low brush as I approached, the horses quickening their pace as they neared the water.

If there were Apaches near they would surely have seen my friends take their rifles and get down among the rocks, and they would be almighty sure to know that meant trouble if they opened fire. But it was a shaky business, a-setting out there on a horse, letting the other ones take the time to drink, and just a-waiting for a bullet.

After a bit I got down, went around the waterhole, and began filling canteens. First off, on coming up to the waterhole I'd taken notice of the ground, and saw coyote, bighorn, and wild horse tracks, and the track of a desert fox, too, but no tracks of anything human. That didn't mean a whole lot. An Apache, if he figured there were white men around, would never go near a waterhole unless he was dying of thirst. He would just hole up some place close by and wait.

One by one I filled the canteens, getting a drink myself in the meantime, and then I mounted up and rode back and took the rest of the horses.

It was an eerie sort of thing, watching the horses dip their muzzles into the water and drink, and listening to that wren in the brush. I could see a place where some javelinas, the wild pig of the desert, had been bedded down.

When the last horse had drunk his fill, I gathered the reins on the black and put a boot into the stirrup. I started to swing up, but something glanced sharp across my eyes and I let go the pommel and dropped.

The bullet, timed for my swing into the saddle, clipped a twig where my head would have been, had I not been warned by that flash of sunlight on a rifle barrel.

On one knee I aimed and fired, my shot echoing those fired by my friends among the rocks, and they all hit within inches of where the Apache had been. Then I was in the saddle and racing the horses back to the rocks. In an instant we were all riding, and another shot hit the sand behind us.

"Only one," Rocca said, "but he'll send up a smoke."

"Maybe we got him," Spanish said.

"We'd have to have luck. We worried him, but I don't think we got him."

We glanced back, and in another minute saw a thin column of smoke rising. We looked at it, but nobody made any comment. The horses were slowed to a walk —they might need to run later. We traveled down an arroyo that left no tracks to speak of, the deep sand obliterating all but indefinite hollows.

We went down across a desert flat and into several parallel ranges of bare ridges, their slopes partly covered with the drift sand. The ridges gave us a little cover, and we stepped up the pace.

The children were very tired now. The endless motion of the horses had lulled them into a state where nothing mattered but a longed-for end of it. As for the rest of us, we lived by the moment, counting on nothing more, knowing that the worst might still lay before us.

Dorset came close to me, and for some time we rode side by side without speaking. Suddenly, about half a mile off to our right, we saw a rider. It was an Apache, but he made no effort to close the distance, simply holding a course parallel to our own. A few minutes later another appeared, to our left.

"They're closing in." Battles lit a cigar, squinting his eyes through the smoke. "I think they've got some place in mind, somewhere up ahead."

Tampico stood in his stirrups, scanning the country around. "We'll turn west," he said.

We wheeled quickly and charged in that direction,

spurring our horses for speed, and drove right at the man on that flank.

For a startled instant I think the Apache had no idea what to do, and then he fled off to the northwest as fast as his pony could carry him.

We kept on west at top speed, wanting to cover ground before they could adjust to our change of direction and pace. We dipped into a hollow dotted with clumps of ocotillo and prickly pear, and charged down it, out of sight of the Apaches for at least a mile. Then we rode up a shallow wash and out on the flat above.

There were at least a dozen Apaches off to the east, riding on a course that would join with ours somewhere ahead. Others were coming up behind, and to the west we could see another party coming along fast to head us off.

Me, my eyes were taking in the country around. We were being boxed. "All right," I said, "we'll run!"

And we ran.

I figure we all knew we were up against it then. They knew we had been swapping saddles, but now they weren't going to give us a chance to do that. They were going to run us the way they'd run wild horses, in relays. If we stopped they'd move in and surround us, so we had to run. And they knew where were were running to.

Oh, they were sly, all right, cunning as wolves. Ahead of us a canyon mouth suddenly opened, a wide, shallow canyon like some of those in western Texas, with sides sloping steeply up to a sheer rock wall about thirty or forty feet high. The Apaches closed in on the sides, driving us into that canyon like into a trap. And we knew it would be a box canyon, with a dead end somewhere up ahead.

"Slow down," I said. "Rocca, we got to find us a place up on the slope, somewhere open to the top."

A shot rang out and one of our horses stumbled, and fell. I swore. Nobody ever likes to see a good horse die, but this one would be eaten by the Apaches.

They had fallen behind now, but they were in the canyon top, which was over four hundred yards wide at this point. There was a thin trickle of water in the bottom, at the east side.

We were almost abreast of what looked like a means of escape before we saw it—hollow up near the rim, a sort of half-basin scooped out by some fall of rock, followed by erosion. Pulling up, I pointed. "We're going up there."

"It's a trap," Rocca said. "We'll never get out of it."

"It's a place to stand and fight from," Battles answered, looking up. He wheeled his horse and started up the slope.

He rode left for about fifty paces, leading the pack horse, then back right, riding a switchback trail he was making himself.

Tampico Rocca was already down behind some rocks, and I dropped beside him. "Go on up," I told Dorset. "At the top you'll have to lead your horse, but keep going."

She was not one to ask unnecessary questions. She knew what Rocca and I were set to do, and she wasted no time. John J. Battles was already halfway up, and he was on his feet, leading his struggling horses. Harry Brook, with one of the Creed boys, was right behind him, but being lighter they could stay on the horses.

Spanish Murphy was waiting, Winchester in his hand, and when Dorset passed him he followed, leading the other horses. They strung out on the trail, making quite a cavalcade.

"Tamp," I said, "there's a steep fall of rock, a sort of watercourse, to the left of where they are going up. It will be steeper but faster."

"Bueno," he said, and looked around at me. "It has been a good race. A very good one, I think."

The Apaches were coming closer—there must have been at least thirty of them. Again I glanced at the slope, checking out the route, the possible cover, the quickest way to the hollow up under the rim. It was farther up there than it looked, and already the others were looking a lot smaller, but they still had a way to go.

One of the Apaches was trying to climb the slope behind us. Rocca tucked the butt of his Winchester against his shoulder, held his aim for an instant, and fired. We saw the Apache slip, half fall, then catch himself and turn his horse away from us.

We waited. The other Indians were scattering out now. We fired, choosing our targets, but we could not see whether we scored or not. But all the Apaches in sight went to the ground.

Rocca ducked back, running swiftly from rock to rock. He was an Apache again himself, swift and daring, yet sure. He paused once, shot quickly, then ran on.

I balanced my Winchester in my hands, took a quick glance toward a bunch of brush and rocks about thirty feet away, and ran for it. A bullet kicked dust just ahead of me . . . another ricocheted off a rock with an angry snarl, a nasty sound; the flattened bullet could have made an ugly wound.

Crawling a dozen feet, and scrambling through the brush, I got up again, rounded a boulder, and was in plain sight of them. I brought my rifle up swiftly. An Apache was running straight toward me when I stepped out, but before he could stop or hunt cover, I squeezed off my shot.

He was not seventy yards away and was facing full toward me, and there was no way I could miss. The bullet caught him running, and he took two steps before he pitched on his face in the gravel of the slope.

Up the watercourse I could hear scrambling feet, and I ran that way. I was taking long strides, leaping from rock to rock like a mountain goat, with lead spattering around me. Once I lost my footing, my heel skidded off a water-worn boulder, and I was pitched into the sand. I came up fast and felt a bullet snatch at my hat as I fired . . . and missed.

The Apache I'd seen was gone. The one I had killed was still lying back there on the gravel.

My breath was tearing at my lungs but I scrambled on up, crawling over boulders, pulling myself from rock to rock. From time to time I was out of their sight.

Suddenly Rocca was right ahead of me. He turned to

speak and I saw the bullet catch him. It dusted him on both sides, and he squatted suddenly on his haunches with blood coming from his side, staining his shirt.

He let go of his rifle and started to fall forward, but I caught him.

Ahead of us was about sixty yards of talus slope, and then the hollow toward which we'd headed.

When I caught Rocca I just naturally let him fall across my shoulders, catching hold of his collar with my right hand. My Winchester was in my left, and I reached down and got a finger through the lever on his rifle and lunged up straight. Then I started up the slope.

That struggle up, with Rocca across my shoulders, my breath most gone, and those bullets coming toward us from behind . . . I never want to do that again.

Somehow I made it, and then stumbled and sort of fell into the hollow. Somebody lifted Rocca off my back, and I saw he'd been hit at least one more time.

Gasping for breath, I stared around me. They were all there, Dorset, the children, Murphy, and Battles, and the horses. And now there was us two.

"The trouble is," John J. Battles said, "we're trapped. There's no way out."

Chapter 13

THE HOLLOW was nowhere more than seventy or eighty feet across, and the side up which we had come spilled over in a slope of broken rock and gravel. Elsewhere the sides sloped up steeply in banks of blown sand and gravel, littered with broken rock from the escarpment above, and dotted with sparse brush. The sheer wall above varied from eight feet in height to twice that.

Our rifles could command the slope down to the canyon where the Apaches now were. With no trouble, one or two men could prevent them from reaching us. On the other hand, if they reached the top of the mesa above us, we could be picked off at their leisure.

My eyes searched the rim. It was cracked and broken, and there were places where a man might be able to reach the top, but no place where a horse could go up.

Dorset was working over Rocca; she had him resting as easy as he could, and she was stopping the blood. Harry Brook, needing nobody to tell him, had bunched our horses at the back of the hollow, out of rifle shot from below. The children were huddled together, watching with wide eyes. Nobody was saying anything, but our situation looked bad. We had water enough for a day, perhaps two.

Slowly, I got to my feet. I said, pointing to the rim, "I'm going to find a way out of this hole."

"Wings." Rocca spoke around the cigarette Dorset had lighted for him. "You would need wings."

"Spanish," I said, "you an' Battles stand 'em off. I'm going up yonder."

They studied the wall. "That's more of a climb than it looks," Spanish said. "But we'd better have somebody up there to hold them back."

I started up the slope, angling across it for easier going. It took all of ten minutes to get to the foot of the escarpment.

On the rock wall I came to one of the cracks I'd seen from below. It was a foot wide at the bottom, widening above to maybe three feet. Here and there a few broken slabs of rock had fallen into it and become wedged. A man could climb out of it all right, but he surely couldn't take a wounded man up that way, so I worked my way along the face.

First thing I saw was a lion track, or maybe it was a jaguar's. There were a lot of those big spotted cats in Sonora; you even saw one in Arizona or California time to time.

The tracks, which were several days old, led right along the face and I followed them, studying every break in the rock that I came to. When I'd gone almost around the basin, the tracks suddenly disappeared.

Now, even a cat, tricky as they may be, can not vanish into thin air, so I contemplated the problem.

That cat had come up from the canyon below, and he surely wasn't going back down. The last set of tracks showed the hind feet dug in a mite, and it looked as if the cat had taken a jump. Then I saw a rock where he might have landed. From where I stood the rock's face was sheer, but the edge, about six feet above my head, was broken, and the cracks were filled with talus.

I realized I couldn't, even by jumping, reach the edge, but when I climbed up on a small rock I could see scratches on the big one I wanted to reach, and there were so many scratches that it looked as if that cat had used this trail a good many times.

Hunting for foot-holds, I found a couple and managed to scramble onto the big rock. There was a crack in the rock that led to the rim in a steep slide, filled with broken rock. In a few minutes I was up on top of the mesa, which stretched away for miles. Here there was thin grass, a few clumps of prickly pear, and the cat tracks, fading away to the northwest.

From where I now stood I could not see the hollow, but only the further rim of the canyon and some of the bottom. There were no Apaches in view, and it was likely none of them could see me.

I went back down into the crack and studied it. It would be a steep scramble, but I'd taken horses up worse places. If I could just get them over that first rock. . . .

As I was easing down bit by bit so as to keep out of sight of the Apaches, I heard a rifle shot from below. That worried me none at all. No Apache was going to climb up that slope with a rifle up there; no Apache was fool enough to try. Chances were some Indian showed himself to test us out and Spanish or Battles let him have one to know we weren't asleep.

What I needed now was to be able to figure out a way to get the folks out of that hole. And it was surely up to me. Dorset and the children aside, the boys with me had come just because they were my friends and knew I needed some help.

That big rock was the thing. There were cracks in it, but none very deep that I'd noticed, so I worked my way back for a closer look. On one side it was cracked and broken, and I began digging at it, hoping to dig out enough so that a couple of horses might scramble up or be hauled up.

First, I pulled out several chunks of rock that were in the crack, big pieces of fifty or sixty pounds. With a call to look out below, I tumbled them over. For almost an hour I worked at it.

The Apaches had taken no action against us, and that gave me hope. None of them had taken off to ride around and get up above us; and as they knew the country, maybe they knew it was miles before there was a way out of that barranca.

Down below me occasional shots sounded, and the

Apaches fired a time or two. The way I was fixed they couldn't see me, nor what I was doing. They knew better than anybody that there was no help I could call on, and no matter what I did they'd have my scalp sooner or later. But I planned to make them work for it. If they wanted my hair they'd have to get it the hard way.

So I kept on at the rock, and unloaded a good many chunks of it.

A long, thin slab formed one side of the crack I was digging into. It was all of six or eight feet long, and must have weighed a ton or more, but as I dug down around it I could see it was a free slab, broken clean off the main rock.

There were a few loose rocks at the base, and I climbed down and pulled them free. I had me an idea now, and I didn't figure to give up on it. In a time and place like that, you gamble on any wild-haired chance. We were boxed in, the Apaches were down below, and they were willing to wait. We had water enough for a while, and ammunition enough for quite a fight, but that wasn't going to get us out of here.

The sun beat down on my back and my shirt was wet with sweat, but I'd never done anything much in my life but work hard, and didn't know any different. Besides, we Sacketts were a right stubborn folk. We just didn't have much give-up in us. We always kept plugging away, and that's what I was doing this time.

Finally, when I'd done what I could in the hole, I climbed up and did what I'd been figuring on. I got into the top of that crack, put my back against one side, and my feet against the other, which bowed up my knees. Then with my hands braced against the rock behind me, I began to push.

The sweat broke out on my face and rolled down me in streams. Nothing happened—nothing at all. I rested a mite and then I tried again. It was on the third try that I felt her give a mite. So I buckled down and tried still another time, and she gave a bit more.

Rocks and gravel trickled down into the hollow below, and then Battles climbed up there to help.

He studied the layout and shook his head. "I don't believe it. Even if you can do it, what then?"

"I figure our number's up," I said. "Not that I don't figure to make them earn it with blood, but that girl now—she's got to have a running chance. She's got to get out, and those children."

He squatted on his heels and looked at me. "So?"

"That little buckskin, now. That's a mountain horse, a mountain mustang, and I figure she could climb a tree if need be. The girl's horse is another. Both of them are small, both are quick and smart. I think we might, if we can make any sort of a way to, get the girl and those youngsters out of here. Might even be a chance for us."

He studied the layout again. If that slab toppled over, it would leave a steep slide of gravel and broken rock. With a couple of husky men pulling and a horse scrambling, it might work. With one horse on top and a rope around the pommel, we might get another out.

Battles got down into the crack and scraped some good footing for himself, and then put his shoulder against the slab. Together we pushed, we strained. Of a sudden she gave. I slid lower to get a better purchase, and we tried it again. She tilted a bit, then stuck. Try as we might, we couldn't push that slab any further.

We backed off and studied the situation, and John J. kept looking at that crack. It was a whole lot wider than it had been, and slanted steeply down to the gravel slope below.

He looked at the crack, and then he looked at me again. "Shall we try it?" he asked.

Well, now. It was almighty steep, but it was all we had. I'd seen wild horses scramble up some steep slopes, but none as bad as this—but with a little help . . .

We went back down into the hollow below where the others waited, and I took a long pull at a canteen. When I looked up to where we'd been it fairly turned my stomach. What we needed was a set of wings.

I saw that they had rigged a little shade for Rocca—
a poncho over a couple of rocks, propped up with a
stick. I went over and squatted down beside him. "I'm
hit pretty hard, *amigo*," he said.

"You'll make it."

He looked up to the rock where I'd been. "What you
got in mind?"

"That's the only way out for the two little horses,
the girl and the youngsters. That girl's got savvy. Get
them out of here, and she's a good bet to make the
border."

"I keep thinkin' of that ranch back yonder," Rocca
said; "of those trees, an' the grass."

"It was quite a place."

"If a man had to die, that would be the best he'd be
likely to find. I figure heaven must be like that. Not
that I'm likely to make it."

He looked at me. "When you going to try it?"

"It's coming on for evenin'. I think we'll try then."

He closed his eyes. "Wish I could help."

Dorset came over and I laid it out for her. We were
going to try to get them out, and she was to light a
shuck for the border, hiding out by day, riding in the
evening or early morning. But she already knew what
she needed to do.

She didn't ask any foolish questions, either. She knew
what was likely to happen here, and she knew what we
needed was a miracle.

"When you get back," I told her, "you might write
a letter to Tyrel Sackett, up in Mora. You tell him about
it. Tell him about Laura, too—how she sent me down
here on a wild-goose chase."

"I'll do that," Dorset said quietly. "When it comes
to that, I may go to see her myself."

"Leave her be. She's poison."

It was no trouble for Dorset, Harry Brook, and the
other youngsters to get to the top. Children are good
at scrambling in rough places, and they took it as a
lark. While Battles stood guard after, it was up to
Spanish and me to get the horses up.

The little buckskin was quick and nimble. She climbed the gravel slope with me leading on the bridle, and though she went to her knees once, she made it. But when I looked up at that crack in the rock, I had my doubts.

Knowing the route, I went ahead, leading the buckskin. Spanish came along behind, but when I climbed into the crack the mustang pulled back and just wasn't having any part of it.

Spanish, he was right behind her, and he took off his sombrero and hit her a lick across the behind. She was almighty startled and gave a big jump, and before she knew what had happened she had her front feet on the crack and her hind feet scrambling for a grip on the slope.

Me, I tugged at the bridle. Spanish hit her another lick with his hat and she scrambled into the crack. There we held up for a mite, to catch our wind.

It was the cool of evening now, with the sky still pale blue in the far-off place where the sun had gone down, but overhead there were a few stars, Sitting back there on a rock, holding the bridle, I took long, deep breaths of that cool air.

All of a sudden the mare decided she wasn't too almighty comfortable standing spread out on the steep side of a hill, so of her own notion she scrambled a few steps higher, then stopped, and we let her be. It was still a far piece to the top.

After we'd all caught our breath we started on, and it was a struggle. But little by little we scrambled up until at last we got on top. By that time it was full dark and we still had the other horse to bring up.

Battles was down there alone, or as good as. Rocca was in no shape to lend a hand, and might be asleep. The Apaches didn't attack at night as a rule, for they had the notion that if a man was killed in the darkness his soul would wander forever in darkness. But if they did try coming up that slope in the dark, Battles could never hold them.

Leaving Dorset with the mare and the youngsters,

Spanish and me made our way back into the basin. By the time we reached the bottom we were so almighty tired we were staggering, and we just naturally caved in.

John J. reported no movement as far as he knew of. Rocca was sleeping. He had lost a lot of blood, and we had no way of treating a wound. Up on the mesa we might find one of the herbs the Indians used, but down here there was nothing.

Spanish worked a hollow for his hip in the sand and went to sleep. After I took John J.'s place, he did the same.

It was still, and overhead the stars were bright as they can only be in a desert sky. A coolness came up from the barranca below, and I listened for any whisper of sound, struggling against my own weariness and the need for sleep. But a few minutes of sleep might mean death for all of us. Only my wariness stood guard, and the thought of them trusting me.

A long while later, Spanish came to me. "You better get a little sleep," he said; "but if we're figuring on getting that horse up the mountain, it won't be much."

There was no need for me to move. I just let go and closed my eyes; and when I woke up it was with a hand on my shoulder.

"They're stirrin' around down there," Spanish said, "and it's gettin' on toward dawn."

"You two hold 'em," I said, getting up. "I'll take that other horse up the mountain."

"Alone? It can't be done."

"It's got to be," I said. "The Apaches will figure it out if we wait. Maybe they already have."

John J. was on his feet, his gun belted on and his Winchester in his hand, a spare cartridge belt draped over his shoulder.

"If it gets bad, pull back to Rocca here, and make a stand," I said. "I'll get back as soon as I can."

He indicated the horses. "Do you think we could make a break for it? Down the slope and right into them, shooting all the while?"

It was a thought, and I said so, but I told him no,

not yet. Then I went and caught up the other mustang and headed for the slope. Oddly enough, Dorset's horse took to it as if it was home country. More than likely she could smell the other horse, and knew it had gone this way. Maybe she could also smell Dorset. Wild horses can follow a trail as good as any wolf—I've seen them do it many a time. And the other horse, with us working to help, had maybe made the trail a little better.

The horse had to struggle, and I tugged and braced myself and pulled, and that game little horse stayed right with it. With daybreak tinting the sky, we made it to the rim.

And then we heard the shots. Somebody down there was using a Winchester.

We heard the chatter of the rifle, then a few slower, paced shots. There was silence, then another shot.

The children were wide-eyed and scared, but they were pioneer youngsters, and no telling the trouble they'd seen before this. Dorset stepped into the saddle and I taken her hand.

"Ride," I said, "and stay with it. Hide out by day, ride by night," I told her again. "Don't shoot unless they get close, and then shoot to kill. I figure you're going to make it. We can hold them a day or two."

She put her hand on mine. "Tell, thank them for me, will you? All of them?"

"Sure."

The shooting down there was steady now. They needed me down there. I knew how Apaches could come up a slope. Nothing to shoot at but a few bobbing, flashing figures, you scarce saw them when they vanished, appeared again elsewhere, and came on.

Dorset knew it, too. She turned her horse, lifted a hand, and they rode off into the coming morning. I taken one look and then I hit the slope a-sliding. Far below I could see the Indians.

Battles was on the rim, bellied down behind rock slabs. Far off, near the stream, I could see the Apache ponies, but nothing was moving on the slope. Behind

Battles I could see Spanish, and he was rolling some
rocks into place, lifting others, making a sort of rough
wall from where John J. was firing to where Rocca was
lying. He was getting set for a last-ditch fight, and the
lay of the land sort of favored our position by being
a mite lower than the rest of the hollow.

Of a sudden an Apache came up from behind a rock
and started to move forward, and my Winchester came
up as if it moved of its own will, and I taken a quick
sight and let go.

High on the slope the way I was, right under the rim,
I had a good view of what lay below. That Apache was
a good three hundred yards off and lower down, but I
held low a-purpose and that bullet caught him full in
the chest.

He stopped in his tracks and Battles shot into him,
getting off two fast shots before he could drop, but when
he did drop he just rolled over and lay sprawled out,
face up to the sun.

A number of shots were fired at me, but all of them
hit the slope a good fifty feet below me, and I decided
right then I was going to stay where I was.

It stayed quiet then, and slowly the afternoon drew
on. Our horses had been bunched by Spanish so that
they were close to Rocca, and the position seemed
pretty good unless the Apaches decided to attack by
night. But I kept on thinking about what we might do.
There had to be a way out.

Now, my pappy was always one for figuring things.
He told me time and again that when in a difficulty a
body should always take time to contemplate. "The
only way folks got to where they are," he'd say, "was
by thinkin' things out. No man ever had the claws of
a grizzly nor the speed of a deer—what he had was a
brain."

Right now we had here a stalemate, but it worked in
favor of the Apache. It worked for him because he had
access to plenty of water and grass, which we did not
have.

And I knew the Apache would no longer wait. He'd

be scaling that rimrock himself, and without horses he could get up there all right, although it would take some doing. We could figure on having them above us by the next daybreak, and then that hollow would be nothing but a place to die in.

We had to make it out of there, and right now. Nobody expects to live forever, but nobody wishes to shorten his time. Of course, a body never knows which turn will shorten it. Like when a bunch of us boys went off to the war we left a friend behind who paid a substitute. We all came back, safe and sound, but the one who stayed home was dead—thrown from a horse he'd ridden for three years . . . scared by a rabbit, it jumped, and he lit on his head. So a man never knows.

Only if we didn't get out of this place we weren't going to be laying many plans.

Up there where I was, I began to give study to the country around.

I knew that getting the rest of those horses up to the top was an unlikely chance. In the first place, most of them were larger and heavier, and altogether harder to handle than the two we had got out. We might just possibly get one horse up, or even two. We would never make three or four.

So I cut that out of my thinking. Somehow we had to get out by going downhill, and that meant riding right through that bunch of Apaches. . . .

Now, wait a minute, I told myself. There to the right . . . that's a slide of sand, but there's a mixed lot of growth in it. There don't seem to be so many large rocks. I studied it as carefully as the light would allow.

If we could just . . . I began to see how we, or some of us, might make it. If we stayed here none of us would make it through tomorrow.

I was going down there right now and face them with it. Only first there was that Apache off to the left. He had been coming up the hill for the last half-hour, creeping, crawling, out of sight more than two-thirds of the time, but always getting closer. Now when he moved again . . .

Settling myself into the sand, I braced my elbow and taken a careful sight. Then I waited. His foot moved. . . . I waited. . . . Then he lunged into view and I squeezed off my shot. He never even twitched.

Chapter 14

WHEN I CAME sliding into the hollow Spanish looked at me. "Was I you, I'd still be travelin'," he said. "It don't look like we're goin' no place down here."

"I've got an idea," I said.

He searched my face. "Well, you Sacketts have come up with some good ones. I hear tell whenever one of you boys are in trouble, the rest come a-runnin'. I'd like to see that now. I surely would."

"They don't know where I'm at."

John J. was stuffing a pipe. He looked haggard and honed down. I hadn't the heart to look at Rocca yet. "What's this idea?" John J. asked. "Right about now I'll buy anything."

"Yonder," I said, "there's a corner of slope that's mostly free of big rocks. There's some grass and some brush, but it's low stuff, and the sand looks as if it's packed."

"So?"

"Come nightfall we mount up. We stampede the horses down that slope into the Apache camp and we go with them. Only we keep on riding."

Battles gave study to it. Spanish, he just looked at me. "How many do you think would make it?" he asked.

"Maybe none . . . maybe one."

Battles shrugged. "Well, it's no worse than here. At least we'd be trying."

"What about Tamp?" Spanish asked.

119

"He isn't getting any better, is he? How much chance has he got here?"

"None at all."

"All right. So we get him into a saddle. You put that Mex on a horse and he'll ride it to hell and gone. I know him. If we get him up in a saddle he'll stay there as long as any of us, dead or alive."

"All right," Battles said, "I'll buy it. What do we do?"

"Pick your best horse. We'll load the pack horse. Maybe he can stay with us, maybe he can't. Maybe he'll follow and catch up. You know how horses like to stay together."

We sat about there, chewing on jerked beef and trying to see all the angles, but there wasn't much we could do but trust to luck. We could hold to the far side of the bunch away from the Apache camp, although that might be the worst thing, for there'd likely be Apaches sleeping around, or watching from everywhere.

Time was a-passing, but we daren't do anything to let those Indians know what we were planning. Saddling up had to be done after dark, and all we could do would be to pray none of them got up on the rimrock before night came on.

Tampico Rocca was lying there with his eyes open when I sat down beside him. "You don't have to tell me," he said. "I heard you talking."

"You reckon you can set up there like I said?"

"You get me into the saddle, that's all I ask. That and a couple of short-guns."

"You'll have them."

We sat quiet then for a quite a spell. It was almighty hot, and even sitting still the sweat trickled down my body. We drank and drank again, and we all ate a little more . . . no telling when we'd get to eat or drink again, if ever.

Finally I taken my rifle and climbed up on the rim. We had to make those Apaches think they had us, and after my helping in two kills from up there, they'd be sure I'd stay there.

Up on the rim I could see no cover for an Apache up there, no way one could come on a man except by night, and if anybody rode from their camp, I could see him.

The camp was too far for a rifle shot, but I could see their cook fires, and see them moving around. Our horses, if we could start them slow, might get within easy distance of their camp before we had to stampede them. And we might be lucky enough to stampede their pony herd, but I wasn't betting on anything.

When it was fairly dark I came down off the rim and we lighted a small fire to make coffee. They knew where we were, and we wanted them to think of us as staying put, although the idea of us trying to break out probably never came to their minds. They knew we were boxed in.

Over coffee we just sat around, keeping an ear tuned for movement. Rocca was propped up by his saddle atop a couple of rocks.

John J. Battles was quiet, saying nothing much until suddenly he started to talk of home. It seemed he'd come from New England, of a good, solid family. He had made a place for himself in the town and was a respected young businessman, and then he got involved with a girl, and another young man from a respected but high-riding family had come for him with a gun. This fellow had been drinking, and threatened to kill Battles on sight. When they met again Battles was armed, and in the exchange of shots, he killed the man.

There had been a trial, and Battles was cleared of the shooting, but he found himself no longer welcome at the girl's house, or anywhere else in town. So he sold his business, went west, and had drifted. He had driven stage, ridden shotgun for Wells Fargo, during which time he killed a holdup man and wounded his partner. He had been a deputy marshall for a time, had driven north with a cattle drive, and scouted against the Cheyenne.

"What happened to the girl?" Spanish wanted to know.

Battles glanced up. "What you'd expect. She married somebody else, not as well off as I'd been, and he got to hitting the bottle. A couple of years later his horse ran away with his rig and he was killed.

"She wrote, wanted me to come back. Offered to come west to me, and you know something? Try as I might, I couldn't even remember exactly what she looked like."

"You didn't have a picture?"

"Had one. Lost it when the Cheyennes ambushed a stage I was traveling on." He paused for a moment. "I'd like to have seen the leaves change color back in the Vermont hills again. I'd like to have seen my family again."

"I thought you had no family," I said.

"I've got a sister and two brothers." He sipped some coffee. "One brother is a banker in Boston. The other one is a teacher. I'd gone into business, but a teacher was what I really wanted to be; only when the moment came I was steadier with a gun that I should have been."

Nobody talked there for a time, and then Battles looked around at me. "Any of your family ever in New England? There was a man named Sackett made quite a name for himself up in Maine during the Revolution. Seems he was wounded or hurt or something, and he spent the winter on the farm with my great-grand-parents, helped them through a bad time."

"Uh-huh. My great-grandfather fought in the Revolution. He was with Dearborn at Saratoga, and he was in Dearborn's command when they marched with General Sullivan to destroy the towns of the Iroquois."

"Likely it's the same man." Battles put down his coffee cup and began to stoke his pipe.

Spanish walked in from the lookout. "All quiet," he said. "There's still one fire goin'."

Quiet as could be, we saddled our horses, and loaded what grub was left on our pack horse. Overhead the stars were very bright, and the night was still. Whilst the others got Rocca ready for traveling, binding his wounds tighter. I crept over to the place where we were going to try to ride down.

The ground was packed pretty good, and there was no slide sand.

The place was narrow, just a strip that might ordinarily have gone unnoticed, except that in our desperation we had looked for any possibility at all. Of course the Apaches might have seen it, too, and might be waiting for us down there, for it was the only place where we could come off the mountain with any speed. But we had not seen it from below, only from the view on the rimrock.

We gathered near the edge, the loose horses before us, held by me and Spanish. Tampico Rocca was in the saddle, John J. Battles beside him, holding our two horses.

It was near the middle of the night when we released our hold on the horses and went back to step into our saddles. "All right," I said, "let's go."

We started the horses forward. We made almost no sound in the night; there was a whisper of hoofs in the sand, a slight creak of saddle leather. I could feel a tightness in my chest, and I gripped hard on the pistol butt in my hand. This would be close, fast work—no chance for a rifle here.

The lead horses disappeared over the edge before us and started down, and as they reached a point about a third of the way down we let out a whoop and each of us fired a shot.

Startled, the half-broken horses lunged into a run. They went down the slope in a scattered band and hit the flat below running all out. A rifle flashed, somebody shouted, and a fire flared up. The Apaches had prepared fires for light, and they lit the wild scene with a dancing glare.

Low down on the black horse, I charged into the night, gun held low and ready. The wind whipped my face, and the horses thundered into the Apache camp.

Off to my left Rocca's gun was blazing. I saw a wild Apache face spring at him out of the dark, saw the flash of the pistol, and the face vanished into the darkness. Somewhere a horse screamed, and I heard a shout from Battles as his horse spilled head over heels, and John J. hit the sand running. I saw him slide to a stop and slam two fast shots at the running Apaches. Then he wheeled and, holstering his pistol as he moved, he made a wild grab at the streaming mane of one of our horses, somehow turned aside from the first rush. He was almost swept from his feet, but he went astride the horse, clinging to his hold on its mane.

Flames stabbed from every side, and then we were through the camp and racing away down the bottom of the barranca.

My black was running all out, and I turned a little in my saddle. Rocca was still coming, riding loose in the saddle, his hat on the back of his neck, held by the string of his chin-strap which had slipped to his throat.

Spanish was off to my right—or so I thought—and we charged on into the night, some of the horses running wild ahead of us, others scattered to left and right.

We raced on, and somehow the horses found a winding trail to the cap rock and slowed to climb it. I called out, but there was no reply. Finally the black struggled over the rim onto the mesa. There was more light there, under the high stars.

I drew up. Here and there I glimpsed a horse, but none that carried a rider.

Slowly I rode on, talking to the horses and hoping the others would follow. Daylight was still far away, but none of us would dare to stop. If they were alive they, too, would keep on.

There was no use to try to find anybody. In the darkness a body could be missed, and any one of us would shy from any other rider for fear he was facing an Indian.

Through the night I rode, once lifting my horse to a trot for a few miles, then slowing again to a walk. I reloaded my gun, checked my rifle. Once, worn out as I was, I dozed in the saddle.

Finally, in the gray light of day, I stopped. Carefully, standing in my stirrups, I looked in every direction. I could see for a good distance on all sides, but there was nothing but desert and sky. Wearily, I started the black horse on again, heading north.

By noontime, with nothing in sight, I got down and stumbled on, leading the horse. There was no telling when I might need all that horse had to make a run for it.

There were no tracks. There was only silence. Overhead a buzzard swept down the sky, returned and circled widely above me. After that he stayed with me, and I figured a buzzard had pretty good judgment about where he might get a meal.

The sun was hot, and no breeze stirred. My canteen had been holed by a bullet and was empty. I stumbled along like a sleepwalker, dead on my feet, yet not daring to stop. Finally I gave up and climbed into the saddle again.

Ahead of me, almost lost in the blue of distance, the cap rock seemed to break off. There were mountains beyond; behind me and to the east there was nothing.

Water . . . I had to have water, and so did my horse. Under a desert sun a man cannot live long without water.

The mesa ended abruptly, but there was no trail to the rough, rolling land below. Here there was another stretch of the rimrock, nowhere less than thirty feet of sheer wall, then a steep, rock-strewn slope.

Far off I thought I could see a patch of green in a fold of the earth. Skirting the cliff, I rode on. Suddenly I saw the tracks of shod hoofs.

The tracks were familiar. They were the tracks of a horse that Spanish Murphy had ridden, a tough, mountain-bred horse, larger than the average mustang, and weighing almost a thousand pounds. Turning into the trail, I followed it along the rim. We came abruptly to a cleft where the rock wall had broken away and there was an easy though steep descent to the valley below. We made it.

We rode on, the black and me, with the black

quickening his pace so as to come up with his friend.
Sure enough, we'd gone not over five miles when we
saw the bay mustang ahead of us. He had stopped, and
was looking ahead, ears pricked.

Well, I shucked that Winchester before you could say
aye, yes, or no, and I eared back the hammer and
walked the black right up alongside that mustang. I
spoke easy to him, and he didn't do more than side-step
a mite, knowing my voice. Then I looked where he was
looking.

There was a thick clump of ironwood beside the way
we were taking, and a horse was standing head down
there, just waiting, and sitting up on its back was a
man. He was sitting there, hands on the pommel, head
hanging like the horse's, and when we started forward,
he paid us no mind.

Good reason why. It was Tampico Rocca, and he
was dead.

Even before I got to him I could see by the blood
on his vest that he'd been shot at least twice, but he'd
lived long enough to lash one hand to the saddlehorn
and tangle the fingers of the other hand in the turns
of the rope.

Rocca had said that if he got into the saddle he would
stay there, and he meant it.

Chapter 15

THERE WAS no need to stay close to him, and I was wary. Had the Apaches seen me coming, it would have been like them to leave Rocca there, and I wanted no traps.

An arroyo offered some shelter, and after a quick glance I rode into it and waited there, listening.

For several minutes I watched Rocca, the horse, and the rocks around. Mostly, it was the horse I watched, for the actions of the horse would warn me if there was anyone close by.

Following the arroyo a little further, I saw a clump of brush and low trees near the lip of the draw, so I rode up the bank in their shelter. After a while, reasonably sure that it was safe, I went back to the horse and its burden.

The trailing bridle had caught in the brush, and I let it stay there while I lifted Rocco from the saddle after freeing his hands. There was nothing with which to prepare a grave, so I found a shallow watercourse, placed him in it, and covered the body with brush and rocks.

But first, I had taken his guns and ammunition, to leave nothing for the Apaches if they found him. There was a full belt of ammunition as well as some loose cartridges. And there was a swallow of water in the canteen.

In his pocket I found a stub of pencil and some old papers on which he had been learning to write his name. He had gotten somebody to write it for him, or had taken it from something addressed to him, and had practiced, over and over again, on many different surfaces. I had never seen him do so, nor likely had anyone else, for he was a proud man, ashamed to let us know he could not write, and that he cared.

There was no address, nothing to show that there was anyone to whom he belonged. But there had been a girl he had talked of, so I took what money he had, only a few dollars and some pesos, to give to her.

Scarcely twenty minutes was used in burying the body. Then, leading the spare horse, I went back to the arroyo and followed it for perhaps a mile, the soft sand leaving no tracks that could be recognized. When I came out I started across country.

The sun had gone down by now and the desert was cool. Off in the distance I could hear a quail call . . . I hoped it was a real quail.

I felt stiff and cold now, and I worked my fingers to keep them easy for my gun. Shifting to Rocca's horse, I rode on into the night. There was no trail, but I went ahead, all the time looking for water. The green place I'd seen from afar should be near.

The black horse pulled up alongside me, and Rocca's horse quickened its pace. They smelled it.

An arroyo opened on my right and I found my way into it, listened, then walked the horses on, knowing the arroyo would end where the water was. The arroyo gaped, and I looked into a small oasis darkening with the cool of evening.

There were a dozen cottonwoods, some mesquite and willows, and slopes green with grass, and through the trees a glimmer of water. I could hear birds twittering. The horses tugged at their bits, wanting to go forward. Winchester in hand, I walked them slowly, ready with a spur if need be.

Suddenly my way was blocked by a low stone wall that looked to be a part of one of those *trincheras* the ancient people built to terrace and till their land, or sometimes for dams. I'd seen a lot of them in Mexico.

Dismounting, I led the horses around it and down to a broken place in the wall, and saw something dark and shadowy through the trees. There was no sound but the water, and the rustle of the cottonwood leaves. I walked ahead to an opening among the trees, and came to an ancient ruin. It had once been a considerable structure, built right from the edge of the pool back to the cliffs where it joined the native rock.

Only the floor remained, and a corner of a wall that reached up to six feet, slanting down to no more than three feet near the water. There was green grass all around, and a stillness that came from utter isolation.

First off, I let the horses drink sparingly, and drank myself, and then filled Rocca's canteen. All the while I kept my ears tuned for any sound. But there were no tracks around that I could see, no signs of campfires, nothing to show anybody had been here at all in years.

Picketing the horses, I found a corner of the wall that protected me on two sides. A pile of fallen adobe bricks mingled with chunks of rock that had been used in the walls formed a partial breastwork on the other sides.

Tired as I was, there was no sleep in me. Places like this made a man sort of sad. Somebody had lived here, and judging by the look of the place, different people at different times. There had once been a building of native stone. It had fallen in and been rebuilt with adobe and rock; and it looked as if the last time was no more than thirty, forty years back. Indians had perhaps built the place first, and rebuilt it, too. Later white people had settled in here until driven out.

It was a quiet place. A small garden patch had been worked at one time, and there was a meadow where hay might have been cut, but nobody could live long in such a place with the Apaches on the rampage.

I settled down, and after a while I slept. I awoke when the morning sun began to filter through the leaves. Everything was as quiet as before. I watered the horses, saddled them, and prepared to move out, but first I had scouting to do.

There were crude steps cut from the rocks at one side, taking advantage of natural steps left by the erosion of rock layers. Climbing these, I found a natural hollow that had been shaped by hand into a lookout of some comfort, with a view in all directions.

For several minutes I studied the desert, but saw nothing. Back down below again, I dug into my saddlebags for the small packet of coffee I always carried for emergencies. Often I carried some jerky and flour, but now there was only the coffee.

I built a small fire, and rinsed out an old clay jar I found. When I'd made coffee I filled a cup and prowled around, and finding some chia, I gathered a handful of the seeds and ate them. Then I went up for another look.

Off to the north I glimpsed a buzzard. There might be a dead steer, or it might be one of my friends, and buzzards do not always wait for a man to die.

Due north I rode, then I swung wide to the east, cutting for a sign. Whatever was up ahead must have left tracks getting there, and I wished to find out what I was up against.

"Tell," I told myself, "you better ride easy in the saddle. I think you're headin' into trouble."

That black flicked an ear at me as if to show he agreed. A lonely man a-horseback in wild country gets to carryin' on conversations with his horse, and some horses become right knowledgeable and understanding.

No tracks. I rode up on the east of where the buzzard circled, and swung in closer. Standing in my stirrups I looked the country over, and at first I saw only a lot of prickly pear around, and some clumps of cholla, all white thorns on top, brown underneath.

Then I saw the horse—a horse down, a saddled horse.

Circling around it, rifle in hand, I taken a chance and called out: "Spanish? Is that you?"

A couple of buzzards roosting in a palo verde tree nearby looked mighty upset with me, and one of them flopped his wings as if to scare me off or stampede my horses.

No answer came back. So I cut a little closer, then drew up and looked around. It was all just as it should be, sunlit and still.

My black was curious, too. He could sense something I could not, and though it made him curious, it was something he shied from. Probably it was the dead horse.

I walked him slowly forward, the hammer of my Winchester eared back for trouble.

The shirt was what I saw first, then the boots, and the Mexican spurs with the big rowels. It was Spanish.

I swung down and, having tied the black to a mesquite, I walked up to him.

He was lying face down in the sand, but he had pulled his saddlebags across his kidneys; so he'd been alive and conscious when he hit the ground. He knew that buzzards went for the eyes and the kidneys first, so he'd rolled on his face and pulled those saddlebags over him. They might not help much, but getting them off him might bring him to enough to fight the buzzards off.

Lifting the saddlebags free, I rolled him over.

There was blood all over the front of him, dried blood that seemed to come from a shoulder wound. And there was blood lower down that came from some place in his middle. But he was breathing.

We were right out in the open, and those buzzards could attract more than me; so, good for him or not, we had to move.

He muttered something, so I tried to let him know who was with him. "It's all right, Spanish," I said. "You'll see that girl in Tucson yet."

There was no time for fixing him up at all. Gathering him into my arms, I went with him to the spare horse and put him in the saddle; then I lashed his wrists to the pommel and his boots into the stirrups. I taken his saddlebags, although what was in them I didn't know. Then I checked his horse, but the animal was dead. There was a rifle in the saddle scabbard, so I took it along. There was no canteen.

We rode out of there at a good clip. The country ahead promised nothing. We had two, three days to cross the border, but we'd not be safe until we got to Pete Kitchen's or to the settlement on the border.

Taking advantage of every chance to mask my trail, and trying to keep down the dust, I rode north, leading Spanish on Rocca's horse. The wind was picking up a mite, which might drift enough sand to cover my tracks, but there was small chance it would be in time. Several times I slowed down, checking animal tracks, and watching for any sign that might indicate water.

The trail behind was empty, and the trail ahead looked clear. I rode in my own small world of sunlight, the movement of horses, and the smell of dust and sweat. Ahead of me, on the right, a sawtooth range showed itself above the flatter country around us.

I slowed my horse to a walk, for there were dark streaks of sweat along his flanks. An arroyo opened ahead of me, and I rode into it and found a way up the opposite bank. A towering butte was ahead for destination.

The bullet smashed against the pommel of my saddle, then ricocheted away with a nasty whine, and the heavy report of the rifle followed. Slapping spurs to my horse, I started to run him as three Apaches broke from cover to my right. They had waited in ambush, but my dip into the arroyo had fooled them and now they came running.

Turning in the saddle, I taken aim as best I might and fired . . . once, twice . . . three times. I saw a horse stagger and go down, spilling head over heels in the sand.

Ahead of me three more Apaches had come from right out of the desert, it seemed. I turned my mount a little away from them and raced on, holding my fire. Behind me Spanish rode like a sack of grain in the saddle, his body lurching with every jump, yet somehow he remained upright.

They came at me, and suddenly I wheeled the black and charged into them, firing my Winchester with one hand as if it was a pistol.

The sudden switch surprised them and one of them turned so sharply his horse spilled into the sand. Another was right ahead of my rifle barrel and not thirty feet away when I shot into his chest, dusting him on both sides. He went down, and then we were through and riding for that butte.

Behind me there was a shot and something tugged at my shoulder, but we were off and away. Sliding my Winchester into its scabbard, I drew a six-gun and fired, slowly and deliberately, trying for a score. The first shot missed; so did the second. Then an Apache elected to swing his horse around a small cedar just as I thumbed back the hammer. He was broadside to me and I let go, heard the slam of the shot, and saw the Apache lurch in the saddle, then swing off to one side, barely clinging to his horse.

Suddenly, from ahead there was the hard bark of a rifle, and glancing back, I saw another Indian falling. I raced forward, scarcely daring to believe it could be help, but the Apaches, wily fighters always, were swinging away. And Spanish was still riding behind me.

The desert fell away in a long slope ahead of us, and on the rim stood John J. Battles, dusty, bloody, his hat gone, his shirt torn. He got up from the ground as we approached and swung into the saddle . . . and he had the pack horse.

"She found me," he said. "Came trailing along the desert, part of her pack gone, the rest hanging under her belly."

"Did you see anything of the youngsters?" I asked.

"No, not a sign." He looked back at Spanish. "He hurt bad?"

"I haven't had time to look. I think so."

We pushed on, praying for the night to hurry, and finally it came. Our horses slowed to a walk, and Battles and me, we swung down to save them as much as we might.

"How far d'you think to the border?" Battles asked.
"Maybe sixty miles," I said. "Might be less."

He stopped to work his toes around in his boots. I
knew the signs, for I was doing the same thing. We
were both almighty tired. I figured I was stronger than
him, and I'd been running on nerve. I seemed to have
been hot, tired, and sore as long as I could remember.
My muscles ached, my eyes hurt from the glare, and
felt all the time as if they had sand in them. I was wanting to stop with every step, and I knew the horses
didn't feel any better.

But we kept on, because neither of us was smart
enough to quit. Finally Battles stumbled and went to
his knees, and he was slow getting up.

"You better get on your horse and ride for it," he
said. "Ride that horse to death if need be, but get to
safety. We just ain't a-going to make it like this."

I didn't answer, but kept on going. Every time I put
one foot ahead of the other I figured I'd gained just that
much. Then when I had stumbled a couple of times
myself, I realized the black horse was tugging at the
bridle. He wanted to go off to the east.

"Mount up, John J.," I said. "Maybe we've found
something, but you hold ready to shoot, because we
may find trouble." I was so dry I had to try twice before I could make the words come.

Once in the saddle, I just let the black have his head,
and that horse started off at a good clip, considering
the shape he was in. And the others came on behind,
Spanish Murphy still a-setting up there like a preacher
pronouncing sentence on Satan, his head bowed but his
shoulders hunched as if he figured maybe Satan was
aiming to get in one more blow.

It wasn't long before we felt a coolness, and the
horses lurched down into an arroyo and all of a sudden
we came up to a small fire where there were four or
five Apaches gathered around, eating a fresh-killed
horse.

No telling who was the most surprised, but Battles
got off the first shot and he drilled one of those Injuns

with meat in his teeth. and the rest of them fell away
into the shadows like so many ghosts. I slammed spurs
to my black and jumped him across the fire in time to
see one Apache snaking into the brush, and I cut down
on him. Something slammed alongside my head and I
felt myself hit ground, bounce, and fall free, losing a
boot in the stirrup.

I rolled over, my Winchester gone in the brush, and
I clawed for a six-shooter. And then I froze right where
I lay, because an Apache was standing astride of me
and he had the razor edge of his blade right across my
throat. He was looking me right in the eyes, and I could
see the firelight on his scarred face, and we knew one
another at the first glance. It was Kahtenny, the Indian
I hadn't been willing to kill, way back there in my fight
with the Apaches.

"You better hold back on that edge," I said. "You're
liable to cut somebody."

Chapter 16

HE STILL STOOD astride of me, that knife edge against my throat, and he never moved it one mite. He kept looking right into my eyes and I looked right back at him, and I knew all he had to do was make one quick slash to end my days.

Then easylike, to give no false notions, I lifted my hand to his wrist and pushed the blade away, very gently.

"That's a good knife. Got quite an edge to it," I said.

"You are brave man. You are warrior."

"We are warriors together," I said. "It is enough for you and for me that we know each other."

The other Apaches were filtering back out of the darkness, and their black eyes were reaching to me in anticipation, I expect, for the torture of a strong prisoner was a pleasure not to be missed.

Right off I recognized Toclani among them. He had served in the army under Emmet Crawford as one of his company of Apache scouts. Toclani and me, we had ridden together, shared our grub, and fought side by side against other Apaches. Now I had no idea whether that would help me any at all, for Toclani might have returned to the wild ones, the broncho Apaches who fought whoever stood in their way.

They had me dead to rights. What lay ahead I knew full well, as any man along the border would know, but what worried me now was what had become of Spanish and Battles. Had they got clean away? Spanish was more dead than alive, anyway, and Battles was neither as good as Spanish or me when it came to desert travel.

Nobody had made a move to tie me, but they had taken my knife and my guns, and there was not much of a chance to run for it. Moreover, I was in mighty bad shape. I needed a drink, and my stomach was growling at the smell of the meat on the fire.

We had accounted for a couple of the Apaches, but there'd been at least a dozen out under the brush before the shooting started, and now they came up to the fire, and kindled another one close by.

I could see my Winchester lying over yonder beside my Colt, but they were thirty feet away and I'd have no chance to go after them. Kahtenny was off to one side, beyond the fire, and he was talking to the others, but I couldn't make out a thing they were saying. All I could gather was that some kind of an argument was going on, and I had an idea it concerned my hide.

While the Apaches ate, at least three of them kept a watch on me all the time, but seeing I wasn't going anywhere anyway, I stretched out and, using my hat for a pillow, I went to sleep.

When I woke up it was maybe two hours later and the fire was down. Most of the Apaches lay around sleeping, and I still wasn't tied, which made no sense at all unless they figured on having some fun when I made a break for it.

Thirst was about to strangle me and the waterhole was right beyond the edge of camp, so I got up, making no special try at keeping quiet, and I walked over to the waterhole, lay down and drank. Then I went back and stretched out again.

I knew as well as anything that at least four or five pairs of eyes had been on me all the while, and had I jumped for a gun or a horse they'd have had me. So I just stretched out quiet, feeling a whole lot better for the drink.

Presently Kahtenny got up and walked over to me and sat down. He rolled himself a smoke as easy as any cowpoke you ever did see, and he sat there smoking until half of it was gone before he spoke.

"Somebody want to kill you."

"Me?" I chuckled. "Maybe a lot of folks." I sized him up as having something puzzling on his mind. "You mean your boys?"

"Other man. White man."

"A white man wants me dead? What makes you think so?"

"He have my squaw. He say, you dead he give her to me. I bring your body, he gives squaw."

"So why haven't you done it?"

Kahtenny looked puzzled. "Why he want you dead? I think somehow it is a trick."

"How'd you get the news? Did Toclani bring it?"

He showed no surprise that I knew Toclani. "Yes ... he bring it. My squaw ... she talk to sister at San Carlo. She go quickly in the night, but when she leave these men take her."

"Did they hurt her?"

"No. Toclani say no." He looked at me. "Me fight Toclani, but Toclani good man. My squaw good woman. Toclani puts Apaches to watch out for my squaw."

"Who are these white men?"

"Their name is Hadden. There are several. Toclani sees them. Why they want you dead?"

"I shot them up. Rocca . . . you know Tampico Rocca? They called him greaser and were going to kill him. We fought. Rocca and me, we kill one . . . maybe two of them.

He still was not satisfied. "Toclani says you good man. Great warrior."

There wasn't much I could say to that, so I kept my mouth shut and waited, but my mind was working as fast as I could make it. I lay no claims to being a thinker or a planner. I'm just a mountain boy who grew up to be a free drifting man, but it didn't take much figuring to see I had a way out of this if I could come up with the right ideas.

Trouble was, I had to play my cards almighty careful,

because I surely didn't have any hole card. One thing working for me was that Kahtenny was suspicious, and feared a trap.

To kill me of his own idea would be simple enough, and likely that's what he would have done, after some torture to see what kind of a man I was. But now somebody else wanted me dead, and he was puzzled.

From what I gathered, Kahtenny's squaw had slipped back into the reservation to see her sister and that was when the Hadden boys caught her . . . waiting until she started to leave.

It was nothing unusual for a wild Apache to return to the reservation, stay a while, and then leave. The Army was always trying to get them to return, and often the squaws would come back first to look over the situation.

Now they had Kahtenny's squaw and he wanted her back, but he was like a wild thing that sniffs trouble at every change, and there was a lot about this offer that he did not like.

He sat smoking and waiting, and finally I said, "I think you can not trust them."

He looked at me. "They will kill her?"

"They are bad men. They would have killed Rocca for nothing. I think if you take my body to them they will kill her and you also . . . if they can."

He waited a while, and I poked sticks into the fire. Then I said, "Give me my guns. I will get your squaw for you."

For a long time he said nothing, then abruptly he got up and went to the other fire, where he remained, occasionally in low-voiced conversation. After a while he came back and sat down on the sand. "You can get my squaw?"

"Kahtenny is a warrior. He knows the ways of war. Much can happen, but this I promise. I shall get her safely if it can be done."

After a pause, I added, more quietly, "The Haddens are not Apaches. They are fierce men, but they are not Apaches. I can get your squaw."

"She is a good woman. She has been with me for many moons."

"Do you know where they are?"

"We take you there. It is near the border."

Nobody needed to warn me that my troubles were only beginning. Kahtenny might use me to get his squaw back, and then shoot me down in my tracks. It wasn't that an Apache wasn't grateful, he just had different ideas than we folks had. If you were not of the tribe you were a potential enemy, and killing you was in the cards.

There had been no sign of Spanish or of John J. Nor in the little I could overhear was there mention of them. It seemed likely that they had gotten clean off. Well, luck to them.

At daybreak they led my black horse to me and I saddled up, taking my time; but when I started for my guns, they stopped me and Toclani took my Winchester and hung my gun belt over his shoulder. They let me fill a canteen, and then we started out.

All the time we were riding I kept thinking about Neiss, who was one of five men on a stage near Stein's Peak when it was hit by Cochise and his band. The driver and a man named Elder were killed right off, the stage capsized, and the men were preparing for a fight when Neiss talked them out of it. Cochise, he said, was an old friend; just let Neiss talk to Cochise and all would be well, so they tried it. Cochise roped Neiss and dragged him up the canyon over the rocks, cactus, and brush, while two other warriors did the same for the others. Then they were tortured to death. That happened in April of 1861.

Thinking of this, I was placing no great faith in my chances with them, and although they watched me like hawks, I kept a wary eye out for any chance of escape.

There wasn't any.

My black horse was gaunt and worn by hard travel. To break and run, even if the chance came, would get me nowhere. I had no weapon and there was no place to go . . . no place I could reach in time.

The sun glared down on us as we walked our horses across the parched, rocky hills, weaving amongst the cactus and the greasewood. It was rolling land, broken by short sawtooth ranges of dull red or brown rock, and occasional flows of lava marked by the white streaks of dry washes. Indians rode on all four sides of me, always alert, always ready.

Nobody talked.

Each step my horse took seemed to be carrying me closer to death . . . escape would be too much luck.

I could expect no help from the Haddens. I had no idea how I was going to get the squaw away from them, and I felt sure they had no intention of letting her go free. Even among good men the depredations carried on by the Apaches had created the desire to exterminate them, one and all . . . and the Haddens were not good men.

Me, I always had great respect for the Apache. He had learned to live off a mighty bleak and hard country, and he had none of the white man's ways of thinking, and you had to reach out to try to understand how he felt and what he wanted to do.

After a while we began to see more cholla, great stretches of it, all pale yellow under the bright sun, with the dark browns and blacks of the old branches down below. Jumping cactus, we called it, because if a body passed too close if seemed to jump out to stick you. The Apaches thinned out to single file as we went through it.

All of a sudden we drew up. Kahtenny turned and pointed out a low mountain ahead of us, off to the east. "It is there they are," he said, "at Dead Man's Tank. They are six men, and my squaw, and they want you."

They wanted me dead.

Though Kahtenny would have killed me without waiting if he figured that would be enough, he was no more trusting of the Haddens than I was. They would get my body, but that didn't mean he would get his squaw.

"You're going to have to give me my guns," I said. "If I ride in there without them, they'll kill the both of us if they can. I figure to handle the Haddens. Without them, the others aren't likely to cut up no fuss."

The funny thing about it was, all day my mind had been miles from that hot desert and back in the hill country of the Cumberland. They say a man's whole life passes before him when he's about to die. I can't say that mine did . . . only those times back in the mountains, so long ago.

All day my mind kept going back to turnip greens, and to wild-hog hunting in the hills on those foggy mornings when the forest dripped and a body prowled through it like a red Indian, scouting for wild hogs to give us bacon to cook with turnip greens in an iron pot.

Me and Orrin used to go out, or sometimes Tyrel, though he was younger. Never knew Tyrel to miss, though on occasion I did.

I'd never seen that country since. Never seen it . . . but I hankered for it. Many a time on the desert I looked up to the stars and wished I was back there, seein' the kitchen door open with its light shining out and me coming up from the milking with my pails full to overflow.

You wouldn't hardly think my mind would be on that now, with the trouble I was in right this minute, but that's the way it was . . . as if I had to give my mind some ease with good rememberin'. So all the time, as we rode along, my thoughts kept going back to that green and lovely country.

I thought of the time I floated down the Big South Fork on a flat-boat to New Orleans, taking what we had to trade—corn, sorghum molasses, and maybe some tobacco. We Sacketts never had much to trade except muscle, because our poor ridge-land didn't raise more than enough to feed us, even if we hunted the forest too. But folks liked to have a Sackett along going down-river through some country where unruly folks were liable to be.

My thoughts came back to where I was, and I saw

that Kahtenny was pointing out the land. "You go," he said, "you go get my squaw."

He handed me my gun belt and Winchester, and I checked them for loads. My mouth felt as dry as one of those empty creek beds.

"You keep an eye out," I said. "Maybe I won't be comin' back with her."

We sat there a moment, and then I held out a hand. "Loan me a spare," I said. "I may need it bad."

Well, sir, he looked at me, and then he taken out his six-gun and passed it over. It was a Navy .44, and a likely piece. I shoved it down in my waistband back of my vest.

Toclani rode up. "I will go with you," he said.

"No, thanks. You stay here. If they see me comin' alone maybe they'll let me get close enough to talk. If they see two of us comin' they might just shoot."

So I spoke to that ga'nted-up black horse and we started down, and back behind me Kahtenny said, "You bring back my squaw."

I'd be lucky to do it. I'd be a whole sight luckier if I rode out with a whole hide.

"All right, horse," I said to the black, "let's go talk to them."

And we rode through the cholla toward Dead Man's Tank.

Chapter 17

THE VAGUE BLUE feather of smoke lifted faintly above the rocks of an old lava flow. I could hear my horse's hoofs strike stone, or his muffled hoof-falls in the sand. I sat tall in the saddle, Winchester in the scabbard, my mind open and alert.

There can be no planning in such a situation. Until a man is in the midst of it, he has no idea of the lay of the land, no idea of how the ones he's going to meet will be strung out. You just have to ride in and handle it by main strength and awkwardness, with maybe the salt of a little luck.

The men up ahead wanted me dead. No doubt they had me in their sights right now. No doubt they were holding off to crow over me a mite, or to see what I had to say. As to that Apache squaw, they didn't care one whit. But the Haddens were new in Apache country, and they had no idea what they were up against. If Kahtenny didn't get his squaw, nobody was riding out of there with a whole skin . . . not if Kahtenny could help it.

There was a little thorny, scraggly brush growing amongst the rocks, but the land around was mostly slabs of broken rock, falls of talus off the slopes, or ridges shoved up through the sand.

Glancing back, I could see two Apaches back there, and only two. That meant the others had scattered out and even now were moving in, getting in position for the kill.

144

Now, I'm a peace-loving man, inclined to easy riding and talking around a fire, and the more Apaches I get around me the more peace-loving I become. Riding up there to those rocks around Dead Man's Tank, I could feel my scalp a-prickling as if it guessed it was going to be lifted.

I taken the thong off the hammer of my Colt, and I rode up a narrow trail through the rocks and looked over into a shallow basin.

Dead Man's Tank lay before me, a pool of water maybe ten feet across, each way. Beyond it was a mite of fire, with the thin line of smoke losing itself in the sky. I could see half a dozen horses, and what might be the ears of a couple more beyond the rocks.

The Haddens were standing wide-legged facing me, and there was a man higher up in the rocks with a Winchester across his knees. Two more were by the fire, and likely another might be somewhere about.

Right beyond the fire was Kahtenny's squaw, and even at this distance I could see she was both young and pretty. She looked straight at me, and I was betting she was counting on Kahtenny to get her loose from this setup.

And then I saw Dorset.

Dorset, and one of the youngsters. I gave a quick look around, but saw neither hide nor hair of the others. Maybe they were dead now, or else were crossing the border to safety.

Arch Hadden was looking right at me, and he was smiling, but there was nothing you'd call friendly in that smile. "Well, look who's here," he said. "That would-be tough Sackett."

"Got a message for you, Arch," I said, resting my hands on the pommel, left hand on top. "Kahtenny is out there, and he wants his squaw."

"We told him to send you dead."

"Must have been some mistake there," I said. "I'm still alive."

"Not for long," the other Hadden said, sounding mighty savage.

"I take it you boys haven't had much doings with the Apaches," I said, "so listen to some reason. No matter what's between you boys and me, you'd better listen real good.

"That Kahtenny is poison mean, and he's a fighter from way back. You see him out there almost alone, but he isn't alone. He's got a dozen Indians in these rocks, and more a-coming. If you want to get out of here alive you'd better turn loose his squaw."

The one in the rocks, he ups and says, "We've fit Injuns afore. We ain't turnin' her loose. That there's a right tasty bit of Injun."

Now I knew the chips were down and their cards were on the table. I was sort of watching everything, thinking about how long it had been since I practiced a left-hand draw, and thinking how they were probably counting on that right hand, far from the gun and resting on the pommel, under the left one. I had done that a-purpose, and was hoping it was going to give me the margin I needed. There was this thing of reaction time . . . it takes an instant to see what's happening and for it to register on the mind and dictate a move.

"If you boys are as smart as I think you are," I said, "you'll let that squaw loose, and the same for the young lady over yonder. You know what will happen if you bother a white girl out here."

"Nothin'." That was the man with the rifle up in the rocks. "Ain't nobody goin' to tell."

"You're forgetting about my boys," I said. "They'll know and they'll be telling the story about now."

"Not Spanish Murphy," Arch Hadden said. "He won't tell nobody nothin'. We found him tied on his horse and he didn't look like he was going to make it, so we shot him. We just naturally finished him off."

Dorset was right behind the squaw now, and I never had any doubts about her doing what was best. That little lady had a head on her shoulders and the chances were that right now she was unloosing the squaw.

I knew I had to stall. I had to play for time. "No use you boys building up for trouble," I said. "Turn

that squaw loose, and the lot of us have got a fighting
chance. We can make it out of here if we move fast,
before Kahtenny gets fifty, sixty Injuns out yonder."

"You ain't got the message," Wolf Hadden said.
"We're goin' to kill you, boy."

Me, I smiled at him. Somehow I had to keep those
boys talking, get their mind off the moment to give
myself an edge. If I was going to do anything at all
against the lot of them, I'd need all I could get.

"Most men who try to fight Apaches only learn by
losing . . . and when you lose a fight to an Apache you
never get no chance to use what you learned. You boys
take my advice and turn loose that squaw, and Kahtenny
might just ride off and leave you be."

"You scared?" That was that one up on the rocks.
He was beginning to get kind of irritating, like a mos-
quito around the ear.

"You bet I'm scared. I've seen these boys work. Now,
I—"

All of a sudden one of those boys yelled, "Arch!
That damn squaw—"

She was loose and she was moving, and she was
moving almighty fast. The man up in the rocks swung
his rifle and when he did I forked out that waistband
gun with my left hand and my shot was a hair faster
than his.

He fired at the squaw and I shot him right through
the brisket, and then swung the gun to Wolf, who was
coming up with a Remington Navy.

Dorset, she suddenly threw herself at the man nearest
her and she hit him right behind the knees. He was
standing on a bit of a slope, and when she hit him he
buckled at the knees and fell forward on the gravelly
hillside.

The man who'd been alongside the fire, instead of
grabbing his gun, turned to lay hold of Dorset, and at
the same time that I cut loose at Wolf I jumped my
horse at Arch.

He made a quick step back to get out of the way,

and a rock rolled under his feet. He fell as he drew, jolting the gun from his hand.

I swung my horse and got in another shot at Wolf, who burned me with one alongside the shoulder. He was just setting up to take a dead shot when my second bullet caught him, and he backed up a full step. My black was on him, and he rolled aside, and I felt bullets whipping around me.

Somehow Dorset had a gun. She fired at one of those boys and then taken out running, the child in her arms, for the pony string.

About that time I saw an Apache up on the slope, and he was shooting down at us. I swung my horse again and went after Dorset.

She wasn't wasting any time, and fortunately they had left a couple of horses saddled. She pulled the draw-string on one of them and swung the child to the saddle, then she went into the saddle herself with a flying leap and we were off, running our horses across that desert like crazy folks.

Maybe we *were* a mite crazy. I had an idea we weren't going to make it, but every jump we took gave us a better chance. Behind us I could hear a fight taking place, and somebody else was running a horse off to the right.

Suddenly the desert split right open ahead of us, a deep cut maybe eight or ten feet across. I saw Dorset jump her horse, and I slapped spurs to mine and that black took to flying as if it was second nature. We both landed safe and swung down into a hollow, raced across it and up the other side, and into a forest of cholla where our horses swung right and left and about through that prickly stuff.

We leveled out in the open and put them to a run; and when we finally got them slowed down we had made it away . . . for now.

Looking back, I could see nothing behind us. We had come several miles, and now we walked the horses under some cedars whilst I unlimbered my Winchester, checked it again, and returned it to the scabbard. Then

I reloaded both my six-shooters. I could remember shooting four to five times, but eight shots had been fired, showing I'd been doubling up. I had no recollection of having drawn the second gun, but I surely had.

When I'd reloaded, I moved alongside Dorset. She was holding the youngster on the saddle in front of her.

"What happened to the others?" I asked.

"They got away. Harry is like a little Apache himself. When those men came up he just disappeared into the brush with the others."

"Let's hope he made it."

The country was changing now. It was much more broken, but there was also more growth. There had been a desert shower, one of those sudden rains that sometimes deluge only a small area and then vanish. This one had left water standing in the bottoms of the washes and in hollows atop the rocks. It had filled the desert tanks, so we watered the horses.

My eyes felt like hot lumps in my skull, and they seemed to move with incredible slowness when I turned to look around. My fingers felt stiff, and I worked them and tried to loosen them up. My mouth was dry, and after I'd drunk it was dry again in a few minutes.

All of a sudden I was dead tired again. All the days of driving ahead, running, fighting, and worrying a way out were beginning to catch up with me. But we started on.

The horses plodded ahead, dazed with weariness. Several times I found myself dozing in the saddle; each time I'd wake up with a start of fear, and look all around. My mind seemed to be in a state of despair. Spanish was dead . . . Tampico Rocca was dead . . . where was John J.?

It would soon be dark, and if we expected to make the border we had to find a place to stop for rest. If it had to be, we ourselves could keep going, but not the horses, and without them our chances were gone.

"Do you think they're following us?" Dorset asked.

"I don't know," I answered, and said no more.

The sun disappeared and shadows gathered in the

folded hills. The sahuaro lifted questioning fingers, stark against the yellow sky. The quail began to talk across the silences, the wind stirred, rustling the dry leaves on the parched brush. Our horses' hoofs whispered in the sand.

A lone coyote showed for an instant, then like a shadow was gone, leaving no more sign than an Apache. A few stars began to appear . . . one bright one was low in the sky, and held steady. Time to time I looked at it, and finally I said, "That there's a light. A fire, maybe."

Dorset turned her head to look. "It's not an Indian fire," she said.

We drew up, and I turned, standing in my stirrups to look back.

"It might be the Haddens," I said.

She glanced at me. "After you finished with them? What you didn't get, the Apaches got. You took two of them, I'd swear. Maybe three."

Well, maybe. I wasn't making any claims. I never was one to file notches on a gun . . . a tinhorn trick.

"Shall we try for it?" I said. "It's closer than the border. And the border never meant anything to an Apache except that south of it he was free of the American troops."

"We can scout it," Dorset answered. She swung her pony and headed toward the fire.

The yellow sky faded into gray and velvety dark. Even before we came up to it, I could see it was an Army fire . . . it looked big because there were three of them in line. It was a Cavalry troop of maybe forty men. We pulled up and I hailed the camp.

"Howdy, there. Is it all right to come in? There's a woman and a child with me."

Silence. . . .

It was a long moment, and I guess somebody was trying to make us out with field glasses, though now there was not much light.

"All right," came the answer. "Ride in. Ride carefully."

I knew that voice. It was Captain Lewiston. Lieutenant Jack Davis stood beside him.

Lewiston looked from me to Dorset Binny. He tipped his hat. "How do you do, ma'am. We have been worried for you."

"I'm all right. Thanks to Mr. Sackett."

"Did you come upon any other youngsters, Cap'n?" I asked. "Harry Brook and the Creed youngsters?"

"They're here, and they're safe. That's why we waited for you."

We walked our horses into camp and swung down. I staggered when I hit ground, and Lewiston was beside me. "Here, man, you'd better sit down."

"Got to care for my horse. You take the lady and the child, Cap'n, I—"

"No." Lewiston's tone was suddenly stern. He turned. "Corporal, take this man's horse. See that it is cared for just as mine is. The others also."

He turned back to me. "Sackett, I regret to inform you that you are under arrest."

Me, I just looked at him. "For crossing the border? Cap'n, Laura Sackett told me her son had been taken by the Apaches."

"She has no son!" Davis spoke sharply. "Sackett, that's a damned—"

Lewiston's voice cracked like a whip. *"Lieutenant!"*

Davis stopped, his face flushed. "I tell you, Captain, this man is—"

"Silence! Lieutenant Davis, I suggest you inspect the guard. Whatever needs to be said to Mr. Sackett, I will say."

Davis turned on his heel and stalked away. "Forgive him, Sackett. He's young and I'm afraid he's smitten by Laura Sackett. He is very proud, and he feels he must defend her honor."

"Let him defend it, Cap'n, but keep him away from me. Him being new to the country I might not shoot him, but I am afraid if he said what he started to say he'd be shy a good many teeth."

"There will be no fighting. You seem to have forgotten, Sackett. You are under arrest."

Well, I just walked over to the fire and sat down. Then I dug into my gear which had been dropped there and got out my cup. Reaching for the pot, I poured coffee.

"All right, Cap'n," I said, "you tell me about it. Why are you arresting me?"

"You are under arrest for murder. You are under arrest for the murder of Billy Higgins."

"Higgins?"

"We found his body out on the Yuma road. He had been shot in the head."

"Among other things," I said, "the Apaches wounded him, and then they shot him full of splinters."

"But you killed him."

"That's right, I did." Carefully, with several men standing about, I told him what had happened that day. Some of it I'd told him before, back in the Shoo-Fly when he told me about Kahtenny.

"He begged me to shoot him. Under the same situation I'd have done the same, more than likely."

"Perhaps." Lewiston looked hard at me. "Sackett, is it not true that your family feuded for years with a family named Higgins? That you hunted each other and killed each other on sight?"

"That was over years ago," I said. "Anyway, I ain't been back in that country since the war. As for this Higgins, I never gave it no thought. It's been a good while since I've had any cause to think of it."

"Nevertheless, Billy Higgins is dead, killed by your bullet. I have to warn you, Sackett, the story is out, and there's considerable feeling in Tucson. Higgins had friends there."

"But I tell you, I—"

"Don't tell me. Tell the jury."

He walked away from me, and I sat there by the fire, a-staring into it. I'd run a long way. I'd fought some hard fights. I'd stood off the Apaches and the Haddens, and now here I was, arrested for a crime that was no crime, but a crime they could hang me for.

And there was only one person in Tucson likely to know about that old Higgins-Sackett feud.

Laura Sackett. . . .

Chapter 18

YOU CAN take it from me that no jail cell is a place for a mountain boy. I was raised up where folks looked to the hills, only up where we came from you hadn't chance to look much higher, we were that near the top of the ridge.

This cell they put me into had one small window, too small for me to crawl out of, and a door that was as barred as could be. When I heard that door clang shut I wasn't at all happy. Only thing I knew, I was going to catch up on my sleep, and at least I could eat. And right about that time I was hungry enough to eat an old saddle, stirrups and all.

Captain Lewiston was my first visitor. He came early in the morning, and brought a chair into the cell with him. He also brought the company clerk.

"Sackett," he began, "I want you to give me the whole story, in your own words. I want to help you if I can. Right now the people are divided. Some want to hang you for killing Billy Higgins, and some want to give you a medal for saving those youngsters."

So I gave it to him. How the bunch of us, unknown to each other until then, had banded together to ride to Tucson.

The story of our fight with Kahtenny's Apaches I repeated for him, as I'd told him the whole story before, except the part about me killing Billy Higgins, which I didn't like to think on. Then I told him about my meeting with Laura Sackett, and her story of the lost boy.

"This much I have learned since your departure," Lewiston said. "Laura Sackett was divorced from your brother, and your brothers and her father had been deadly enemies."

"If I ever heard of that, I'd forgotten. We Sacketts were never much on talking of troubles when we were together. It never does any good to go worrying your thoughts about things gone by."

"I approached her last night about your story," Captain Lewiston said. "She denies ever mentioning a child to you, or giving you any cause to ride into Mexico."

I just looked at him. It was no use to say she was lying, although she surely was.

"As a matter of fact, she says you ran away to Mexico for fear somebody would discover you had taken advantage of an Apache attack to kill Higgins."

"Those boys I was with knew better. Why else would they come with me?"

"I am afraid that won't help you at all. I believe you told me that they are dead."

"I buried Rocca with my own hands. Spanish Murphy was finished off by the Haddens. By their own say-so. John J. . . . well, I guess he never made it that far."

"You have no witnesses then?"

"No, sir. Nary a one. You see, Cap'n, none of those men saw it anyway. When I shot Billy Higgins there was just him and me. Nobody was close enough to hear what was said."

Well, we talked a while, and he asked a sight of questions, but after that neither of us had much hope. That feud was ten years out of my mind when I met those men in Yuma, and the name Higgins meant nothing at all to me.

So here I was in jail, and Laura Sackett, who'd been the cause of the deaths of at least three good men, was walking free.

After the captain left I sat on my cot and stared at the blank wall, trying to see my way clear, but nothing came to me; so finally, tired as I still was, I rolled over on the cot and went to sleep.

When I opened my eyes again it was nigh on to sundown and the jailer was at the door.

"Lady to see you," he said.

"All right." I got up, staggering with sleep and trying to get my bearings. This would be Dorset, I figured.

Only it wasn't. It was the last person in the world I expected—Laura Sackett.

She turned to the jailer. "May I talk with my brother-in-law alone?"

When the jailer had gone, she turned those big blue eyes on me.

"I never expected you to get back," she told me coolly, "but I am glad you did. Now I can see you hang, with my own eyes."

"Now that isn't what you'd call neighborly," I said, determined not to let her get any more satisfaction than I could help.

"I only wish Orrin could be here to see you hang," she said, staring at me. "And Tyrel . . . I hated him the most."

"Maybe that's because you couldn't fool him," I said. "But ma'am, do you really want to see me hang that much? I never did you any harm. Never even saw you until I came up the trail from Yuma."

"I want to see you hang, and I will. I only wish I could see Orrin's face when he gets the news."

"Maybe you will see him," I said. "Orrin's a right good lawyer. If he can be free of his duties that long, I'll maybe get him to defend me in court."

She did not like that. Orrin was a mighty impressive figure of a man, and he could talk. He had the Welsh gift for talking, and she knew how persuasive he could be.

"He'll never get here. If you send for him I'll get Arch Hadden to kill him."

"Arch? So that's why he was in Mexico, a-hunting me? I wondered how he knew we'd be there, when we were so all-fired careful that nobody knew."

"Yes, I sent them after you. And I'll send Arch after Orrin, if he comes here."

"So Arch is in town, is he?" That was something to consider, and of a sudden those prison walls began to seem as if they were crowding in on me. Arch Hadden would know I was in jail, and he would come for me. I glanced at that high-up window, and was suddenly glad it was so small and so high up.

"Send for Orrin. I would like that. I will have him killed." As she spoke it seemed to me there was something in those blue eyes that looked mighty like insanity.

"You mistake Orrin. He won't kill easy, and Arch Hadden never saw the day he could draw with Orrin."

I was talking to the wind. She didn't hear me and would have paid it no mind if she had, for I knew she had no such idea as them drawing against each other. She meant a rifle from a hilltop at some stage stop, or something of that kind.

After she had gone I studied about it a mite, and then called the jailer.

"You get word to Cap'n Lewiston, will you? I got to see him."

"Sure." The jailer eyed me thoughtfully. "Did you really shoot that Higgins feller?"

"If you were lying out in the glare of the sun, and you were gut-shot and dying and the Apaches were shooting flaming slivers of pitch into your hide, wouldn't you ask to be shot?"

"That the way it was? I heerd he was an enemy of yourn."

So I explained about the old Higgins-Sackett feud. And I said again, "But I haven't given thought to that fight in ten years, Besides, when a man's hunkered down on a ridge alone, and the Apaches are around him, do you think he'd waste a shot to kill a man the Indians were sure to get?"

"No, sir, I surely don't," he said.

He went away then, and I was alone until the door opened and Dorset came in. She was carrying a plate all covered over. "The lady over at the Shoo-Fly sent this," she said. She lifted her chin defensively. "I didn't have any money or I'd have brought something for you."

"You've done enough. How about you and your sister? Have you got a place to stay?"

"With the Creeds. They'll be coming to thank you. Dan Creed said he'd bust you out of here if you wanted."

"I'll stay. Maybe I'm a fool, but no Sackett aside from Nolan ever rode in flight from the law."

We talked for a spell, and then she left. The jailer returned, but he'd not seen hide nor hair of Captain Lewiston. Lieutenant Davis had been walking out with Laura Sackett, so he had avoided them.

Alone again, I did some right serious thinking. Tampico Rocca and Spanish Murphy were dead. Battles probably was, but even had they been alive there was nothing any of them could tell that would speak for me, because when I shot Higgins I was alone. I'd been a fool to mention it to Laura, but it lay heavy on my mind, and at the time I figured her for family.

What really stood against me was that I'd shot a man who carried the name of a family against which my family had feuded. The man had been wounded several times before, but there was only my say-so that the Indians had done it. The pitch-pine slivers was Apache work, nobody denied that. But the way the talk was going made it seem as if I'd taken advantage of Apache trouble to kill an old enemy, and a thing like that is hard to down.

Billy Higgins had a sight of friends around Tucson, and nobody there knew me except by name. A good part of the talk going around was carried on by Lieutenant Davis, who believed whatever Laura told him.

Two days passed slowly, and I just sat on my cot, and played checkers with the jailer. One thing had changed. That jailer never went off and left me alone any more, and he kept the door to the street locked.

The sheriff was out of town, and wasn't due back for a week, and I began to get the feeling that the quicker they tried me the better. If they didn't hurry, some of those boys outside might be figuring on a necktie party. I began to wish for the high-up country away out yonder, where nobody goes but eagles and mountain sheep. By the wall outside the cell I could see my own outfit—my saddle, bridle, and saddlebags, my rifle and pistol belt. I wanted a horse between my knees, and a Winchester.

Dan Creed came to see me. The jailer knew him and admitted him without hesitation. "You'd better let me get you a gun," Creed said when the jailer had gone back to the office. "They're surely figuring on stringing you up. I've talked until I'm blue in the face, but they pay me no mind. They say, 'sure, he brought your youngsters out of Mexico. You'd speak for him no matter what kind of a coyote he is.'"

"What else are they saying?"

"Well, they say they've only your word for it that the Apaches were still there when you shot Higgins. They say when the Injuns pulled out you just figured to be rid of another Higgins."

Lewiston, who seemed to have been my friend, was gone. Even if I could get word to Orrin and Tyrel, they were too far away to do much good. It began to look to me as if my number was really up.

In matters such as lynching there's always toughs who are ready for it, and there are always people who don't want to be involved. There are men who would stop such things, but it takes a strong man who will make the attempt. I'd never expected to be on the end of the rope myself, although anybody who packs a gun runs that risk.

Again night came, and outside I could hear the mutter of voices, and angry talk. There was no telling if it would come to more than talk, but lying on that prison cot in the darkness I wasn't willing to bet on it.

Suddenly, from out of the darkness outside my window, a voice spoke. "We're going to get you, Sackett. We're going to see you hang!"

My feet swung to the floor, and I was mad clear

through. "Come an' get me, Yellow Belly," I said. "I'll know your voice when I hear it. You just come asking, and you'll get it!"

There was a grate of boots on gravel, and a sound of retreating footsteps.

Suddenly I realized that I was no longer tired. I'd come to this place physically exhausted, but now I'd had three good days of rest, and I was ready. I got up and went to the bars.

"Jim!" I hailed the jailer. "Come running! I got to see you!"

There was no answer, and I yelled again.

There was still no reply. But I heard a mutter of voices.

The jailer was gone, and they had come for me.

Chapter 19

TUCSON WAS for the most part a town of law-abiding citizens. I knew that, and so did that crowd out there. The trouble was, would those citizens get here in time to help me? I knew what those men outside wanted most was quiet, but I aimed to see they didn't get it.

Getting up from my cot, I gave a look around. There was nothing there that would make a weapon except the frame of the cot, which was of half-inch pipe. So I just wrenched the cot clear of the wall, breaking it enough to unscrew two sections of it, one about seven feet long, the other an end piece that was about three feet in length, with an elbow on it.

Standing both pieces close by, I waited. Outside I could hear somebody by the window; then the door from the outer office opened into the prison section. Men came crowding through, and I could see others in the office.

I stood up then. "You boys huntin' something?" I spoke careless-like. "If you are, you've come to the wrong place."

"We're a-goin' to hang you for killin' Billy Higgins."

"I killed him—he asked me to. In his place or mine, you'd have done the same."

I could smell the whiskey on them. This bunch had been drinking to get up the nerve to come after me, but they were tough men nonetheless. I heard somebody fumbling with keys, and knew there was no time to lose.

"I'm going to tell you once, and that's all," I said.
"You boys get out of here, an' get fast."

They'd come without a light, and it was dark as a pit
in there. They hadn't figured they'd need a light to take
me out of the cell, and they didn't want to draw any
more attention than need be. I was only one man and
they were twenty.

"Look who's givin' orders!" somebody said. "Get that
lock open and let's get him out of here!"

Now, there's a time for talk and a time for action,
and I never was much gifted with oratory. I picked up
the long pipe, and when I heard them trying to get the
key into the lock I gripped that pipe with both hands
shoulder high and, holding it tight, I jammed it between
the bars. At close quarters and in the dark it was a
terrible weapon. The passage outside the cells was narrow and they were packed in tight.

With all the power that was in me, I jammed that
pipe into the crowd beyond the bars. I heard the crunch,
then a horrible, choking scream.

"What was it? What happened?" somebody yelled,
and there was panic in the voice.

Drawing back on the pipe, I held it waist high and
jammed it through again, further into them.

Another scream, then a cry, "Back! For God's sake,
let us out of here!"

Somebody else yelled, "What's the matter? You gone
crazy? Let's get him!"

Jerking the pipe back, I smashed hard at the voice
and heard a scream. Then came a shout, "Get out! Get
out!"

Men were fighting and struggling to get out of the
narrow passageway. Thrusting my pipe through the bars
this time at ankle height, I heard several of them go
sprawling. Somebody jerked a gun and fired blindly
through the bars, the shot missing me by several feet. I
drove my bar at the flash and heard a grunt, then
anguished cries of pain, and stampeding feet. Suddenly
the passage was empty except for somebody who lay
groaning on the floor.

"Serves you right," I said calmly. "Whoever you are, you got what you had coming."

"Help! For God's sake, help me!"

"How am I going to do that?" I said. "I'm behind bars. You just crawl outside and get some of those murdering friends of yours to help."

There was another shuddering groan and I heard the sound of dragging. I stood my pipe against the cell wall, and waited. If they came again it would be to shoot, but I had a hunch they wouldn't come.

Now I heard angry questions outside in the street, and then the outer door opened. A match scratched and somebody lit the lamp. Men appeared in the passageway. One of them was Oury, whom I knew to be a reputable man.

"What's happened? What's going on here?" he said.

A man was lying on the floor, and a trail of blood showed where another had dragged himself. A loose coil of rope and a six-shooter lay just outside the cell.

"Seems I had visitors," I said, leaning on the bars. "They wanted me for a necktie party. Only I didn't think it ought to go on without some sort of official plannin', so those folks, they taken off."

Oury's face was grim. "I am sorry, young man. Those were a bunch of drunken teamsters and drifters, not citizens of Tucson."

"I figured as much," I said. "Mr. Oury, do you reckon you could get somebody to bring me a pot of coffee from the Shoo-Fly, and something to eat? I'm getting almighty hungry."

"I will do more than that. Jim"—he turned to one of the others—"get me the keys. I am taking this young man to dinner."

He looked around again. The man lying on the floor was being examined. The doctor looked up. "This man has three broken ribs and a punctured lung," he said quietly.

"That's his problem," I said harshly. "Anybody who fools around with the bandwagon is likely to get hit with a horn."

"Those are my sentiments," Oury said crisply.

The keys jangled, the door swung wide. "Come, Mr. Sackett, you are my guest."

"I don't mind if I do," I said, "but I warn you, I'm an eating man, just getting my appetite back."

The Shoo-Fly was almost empty when we went in, but a few minutes afterward it was crowded to the doors.

When I'd eaten, I sat back in my chair. One of the Tucson citizens came in with my Winchester and gun belt. "If you're staying in town," he said, "you'd better go armed."

"I am staying," I replied, "until this matter is cleared up. I did nothing wrong out there. I killed a good man, a tough man. He might have lived for hours in that boiling hot sun with those slivers burning into him. He was not a man to die easy."

"I might have asked for the same thing," somebody said.

I was quiet after that. I'd eaten well, and I had my guns on again, and all I wanted was to get this affair cleared up and pull out for Tyrel's outfit in New Mexico. As for this town, it was no place for me until my enemies had drifted, and being drifters, I knew they'd soon be gone.

The doctor came in and gave me a hard look. "I'll say this for you," he said, "you're a bad man to corner. You've put four men in bed. One of them has a smashed cheekbone, his face is ripped open, and he's lost nine teeth. One has a torn shoulder muscle, another has a dent in his skull and his scalp is ripped right across the top, laid open for five inches. The one with the punctured lung will live if he's lucky. All said and done, you put four men out of action, and injured six or seven more."

"They came after me," I said.

The outer door opened then and two men came in. One was Captain Lewiston, the other was Toclani, the Apache scout. They looked around until their eyes spotted me, and they came over to my table.

"Sackett," Lewiston said, "Toclani has talked to Kahtenny. They verify your story. Kahtenny told us in detail, as did several other Apaches, what was happening out there during the attack when you shot Higgins."

"You talked to Kahtenny?" I asked Toclani.

"He, too." He indicated Lewiston. "We ride together to Apache camp."

I looked at Lewiston. "You taken a long chance, man."

"It was simple justice. I knew that the people who would surely know what happened were the Apaches. I did not know they would talk, but Toclani came with me, and Kahtenny had much to say of you, Sackett. He said you were a brave man, a strong man, and a warrior."

"Did he get his squaw back?"

"Yes, and he thanks you." Lewiston looked at me. "He may come in. All because of that, he may come in."

"I hope he does," I said. "He's a good Indian."

And so it was over. Nobody wanted me back in jail any longer, but I figured to stay around until the sheriff came back so as there'd be no argument. Around town folks stopped to speak to me on the street, and several thanked me for bringing the youngsters back.

But I saw nothing of Laura . . . had she left town? Or was she still there, waiting, planning?

My mind kept turning to Dorset. Although it was in my thoughts, I'd no right to go a-courting, for I'd no money and no prospects worth counting on. Mr. Rockfellow, who had a herd he wanted pushed over into the Sulphur Springs Valley, hired me and some other hands, but it was a short job, and left me with nothing more than eating money.

The sheriff came back to town, and after hearing what had happened he gave me a clean bill on the charges against me, so I figured to saddle up and show some dust, only I hadn't enough cash to lay in supplies to take me anywhere.

Then at the Shoo-Fly I heard that Pete Kitchen had located himself a mining claim down in the Pajaritos, so I rode down. When he found out I was a hand with a pick and shovel, as well as with a cutting horse and a rope, he hired me for the job.

When he was laying out the grub for me to take along he put in a couple of hundred rounds of .44's. "With your kind of luck, and that being Injun country, you're liable to need them."

Well, I almost backed out. I'd had my fill of 'Pache fighting, and wanted nothing so much as a spell of setting and contemplating.

The Pajaritos are not much when it comes to mountains. They are named for an odd birdlike formation on the butte. I rode down there, leading a jack mule, and I found the mining claim.

There was a wash where run-off water had cut down among the rocks and laid bare some ore. It wasn't of much account, but gave promise of growing richer as it went deeper.

On the back side of a knoll, partly screened by brush and boulders, I made me a camp. On some rough grass nearby I picketed my stock. Then I sat down to contemplate what lay before me.

Now, I'm no mining man, but you don't prospect around, work in mines, or even loaf around mining towns without picking up some of the lingo as well as a scraping of information.

This whole place was faulted. Movements of the earth in bygone times had tilted and fractured the crust until you had a good idea of what lay under you as well as in front of you. The gold, what there was of it, occurred in quartz veins. It looked to me like what they call a cretaceous bed that had rested on diorite, but some of the dikes that intruded offered a chance of some likely ore.

My job was to cut into that, do enough work to establish a right to the claim for Kitchen, and maybe explore enough so as he'd have an idea what lay below. Doing the work I was going to do wasn't going to help much, but I wanted to do the best job for him I could. I never did figure a man hired to do a job should just do it the easiest way. I figure a man should do the best he knows how. So I taken up my pick and went to work on that bank.

While I had a little blasting powder and some fuse, I had no notion of using it. Blasting makes an awful lot of noise, enough to bring every Apache in the country around, and I hoped to do my work quietlike, by main strength and awkwardness, and then pack up and light a shuck for Kitchen's ranch.

After working a couple of hours I sat down to take some rest, and began to notice the bees. Some had gone past while I was working, and now I noticed more of them. I left my pick and shovel and, taking up my Winchester, which I kept ready to hand, I went off up the mountain. Just over the shoulder of it I picked up tracks of a desert fox, just enough to indicate direction.

Between occasional tracks and the bees, I located a rock tank, nigh full of water. Two streams of run-off water coming down off the butte had worn places in the rocks. With a branch from an ocotillo, a dead branch I found nearby, I tried to measure the depth of water in the tank. I touched no bottom, but it was anyway more than six feet deep . . . water enough for my stock and me. It was half hidden under an overhang, and the water was icy cold and clean.

Next morning, after a quick breakfast, I got at my work again. Here and there I found a good piece of ore which I put aside. Now I was doing the same thing most prospectors do. I was putting aside the best pieces, an easy way to lead others to invest, and to lead yourself into believing you've got more than you have. Using water from the tank, I washed out a couple of pans from the dry wash below the claim and picked up a few small colors, nothing worth getting excited about. Unless that vein widened out below where I'd been digging, it was going to cost Pete more to get the gold than it was worth.

By nightfall the cut I'd made was beginning to look like something. I'd sacked up three sacks of samples and had crushed a few of them and panned out the fragments, getting a little color.

The next two days I worked from can-see to can't-see, and had enough done to count this as a working claim. One more day for good measure, and I would saddle up for Tucson.

This spell had given me some time to think, and it showed me there was no sense in saddle-tramping around, riding the grub line or picking up a day of work hither and yon. It was time I settled in for a lifetime at some kind of job, or on a place of my own.

It meant hard work, and lots of it. Living a life is much like climbing mountains—the summits are always further off than you think, but when a man has a goal, he always feels he's working toward something.

The next morning, when I'd been working an hour by sun, I hit the pocket.

It was a crumbling ledge of decomposed quartz, seemingly unrelated to what was on either side, and the piece that I found was no bigger than an upright piano, but it seemed to be only the top of a larger ledge. Anyway, in the next three hours I broke up enough of that quartz to get out maybe two thousand dollars' worth of gold.

Pete Kitchen was going to be almighty pleased. I dumped one of my other sacks back in the hole and filled the sack with the rich stuff. I was just loading the last of it and was too busy to be rightly paying mind to anything else when I hear a voice saying, "Looks like this trip is going to pay off mighty handsome."

Laura Sackett was there, and three men were with her—Arch Hadden, Johnny Wheeler, sometime gunman for a smuggling outfit, and one of the gents who had been with Hadden in the fight at Dead Man's Tank.

They had come down here for only one reason, and that was to kill me, and they wanted to tell me about it. There was no call for conversation, not having to stall like before, so I just peeled back my forty-five and wasted no time.

I turned and saw and drew and fired, all kind of in one breath. My first shot took Johnny Wheeler, whose hand was lingering around the butt of his six-gun as if he was minded to use it.

That shot hit right where the ribs spread apart. My second shot was for Arch Hadden, but it missed. Arch had suddenly whipped his horse around and was running like all get-out.

Laura's horse reared up and she toppled from the saddle, and of a sudden the other gunman was shooting past me. I turned to see the Apaches coming down and recognized one of them as Kahtenny.

Me, I dove into that hole I'd been digging and had sense enough to grab the picket ropes of my horses, which I'd had up, loading for the homeward trip.

The Apaches swept by and I saw that third gunman go down. I heard the bark of Apache guns and saw the dust jump from his vest. He came up shooting, only another bullet nailed him.

They caught Arch Hadden.

I saw them catch him. It was Kahtenny and two others, and I saw him turn to fight as they rode up, but a rope sailed out, and then another, and the Apaches had themselves a prisoner.

Well, I'd told him. He had stolen Kahtenny's squaw, and he had been warned. With Apaches, nothing much was doubtful from here on—only how long Hadden had the guts to stick it out.

This was a hard land, and the rules were written plain in the way we lived. If you overstepped the rules you had bought yourself trouble, and from now on it was going to be settled between Hadden and Kahtenny.

Me, I got up and went to my horses. I fed shells into my six-shooters again, and then I walked over to the man I'd shot to see if he was alive. He wasn't. Johnny Wheeler was buzzard meat.

I taken his guns off, and what he had on him for identification. Might be somebody, somewhere, who'd be wishful to know what happened.

And then Laura Sackett got up off the ground and we just looked at each other. I never did see such hatred in anybody's eyes.

"Downright mis'rable, ain't we?" I said calmly. "You'd think one of us Sacketts would be considerate enough to die so's you could get some of that bile out of your system."

"I suppose you're going to kill me?" she said.

"No, I ain't. It would be a kindness to the world, but I never shot a woman yet, and don't figure to now. No, I'm just goin' to leave you. I'm just goin' to mount up and ride right out of here."

"You'd leave me here?" She was incredulous.

"There's a horse yonder. You get on that horse and ride."

Putting my foot in the stirrup, I swung into the saddle, and you can just bet that before I swung a-straddle of that horse I swung the animal around so I could keep an eye on her whilst I was doing it.

I taken a turn around the saddlehorn with the lead rope of the pack horse, and she said, "What if those Indians come back?"

"It's their tough luck, ma'am," I said, "but I hope not, for their sakes. Apaches aren't bad folks. They have trouble enough without wishin' you on them. Only it might work out for the best. A session with some of those Apache squaws might teach you some manners."

I touched my hat. "I hope I won't be seein' you, ma'am. Good-bye!"

That black of mine went down into the arroyo as if he knew what was behind him, and when he topped out on the rise beyond we were out of rifle shot. I pulled up then and looked back.

She had caught one of the horses and was trying to mount. The horse was worried by her skirt, and was sidling around.

That was the last I saw of her, of Laura, who had been Orrin's wife.

I rode east, with the sun going down behind me, the feel of a good saddle under me, and a horse between my legs. The trail dipped into a wide hollow, shadowy with evening, and somewhere a quail called. Across yonder hills, miles away, was Pete Kitchen's. I'd make camp before I got there, because nobody in his right mind rode up to Pete's in the nighttime.

He was paying me twenty dollars for the job, and might cut me in for some of the profits. Anyway, it was a road stake, and maybe before lining out for somewhere across the country I'd just ride around and call on Dorset.

I liked that little girl. She was pert and she was pretty, and she had nerve.

A star came out, the desert night was soft, and a coolness came over it.

It came on me to sing, but my horse was carrying me along nicely, and I was not wishful for trouble.

ABOUT THE AUTHOR

LOUIS L'AMOUR, born Louis Dearborn L'Amour, is of French-Irish descent. Although Mr. L'Amour claims his writing began as a "spur-of-the-moment thing," prompted by friends who relished his verbal tales of the West, he comes by his talent honestly. A frontiersman by heritage (his grandfather was scalped by the Sioux), and a universal man by experience, Louis L'Amour lives the life of his fictional heroes. Since leaving his native Jamestown, North Dakota, at the age of fifteen, he's been a longshoreman, lumberjack, elephant handler, hay shocker, flume builder, fruit picker, and an officer on tank destroyers during World War II. And he's written four hundred short stories and over fifty books (including a volume of poetry).

Mr. L'Amour has lectured widely, traveled the West thoroughly, studied archaeology, compiled biographies of over one thousand Western gunfighters, and read prodigiously (his library holds more than two thousand volumes). And he's watched thirty-one of his westerns as movies. He's circled the world on a freighter, mined in the West, sailed a dhow on the Red Sea, been shipwrecked in the West Indies, stranded in the Mojave Desert. He's won fifty-one of fifty-nine fights as a professional boxer and pinch-hit for Dorothy Kilgallen when she was on vacation from her column. Since 1816, thirty-three members of his family have been writers. And, he says, "I could sit in the middle of Sunset Boulevard and write with my typewriter on my knees; temperamental I am not."

Mr. L'Amour is re-creating an 1865 Western town, christened Shalako, where the borders of Utah, Arizona, New Mexico, and Colorado meet. Historically authentic from whistle to well, it will be a live, operating town, as well as a movie location and tourist attraction.

Mr. L'Amour now lives in Los Angeles with his wife Kathy, who helps with the enormous amount of research he does for his books. Soon, Mr. L'Amour hopes, the children (Beau and Angelique) will be helping too.